Shattered

Julia Vellucci

Ukiyoto Publishing

All global publishing rights are held by

Ukiyoto Publishing

Published in 2022

Content Copyright © Julia Vellucci

ISBN 9789359209685

All rights reserved.
No part of this publication may be reproduced, transmitted, or stored in a retrieval system, in any form by any means, electronic, mechanical, photocopying, recording or otherwise, without the prior permission of the publisher.

The moral rights of the author have been asserted.

This is a work of fiction. Names, characters, businesses, places, events, locales, and incidents are either the products of the author's imagination or used in a fictitious manner. Any resemblance to actual persons, living or dead, or actual events is purely coincidental.

This book is sold subject to the condition that it shall not by way of trade or otherwise, be lent, resold, hired out or otherwise circulated, without the publisher's prior consent, in any form of binding or cover other than that in which it is published.

Dedicated To:

Those who feel like the side character or villain. You may appear that way in the stories of others but you know yourself and your worth better than anyone else. Redefine yourself in your story. I hope this book can teach you that your story belongs to nobody other than you and those you choose to live it with.

Acknowledgements

Many thanks to those who began to tell fairytales long before there was a name for those stories. These tales taught us lessons, kept us hopeful and truly have inspired me. However, certain aspects of fairytales can be one-sided. The villain suffers at the end of each story, yet in real life, those who appear to be bad often don't face those consequences. One might say that the world isn't fair but I think it's because they are misunderstood; weren't always the way they were and deserve another chance. Don't get me wrong, the idea of love having no limits or the damsel's knight in shining armour always being there at the right place and time can make us look forward to everlasting connections. Yet sometimes love challenges us constantly to truly value it before we realize that it has no limits for those meant to be in our lives. Even knights aren't always there to save us for the right reasons. Some may be lucky enough to not realize this or understand it vaguely until all is perfect yet again. But for those who constantly deal with challenges and phony knight after knight, their walls they keep up as protection or how they unleash their locked up emotions can be frightening and almost villain-like.

Never forget that we're all human, living the same story as we're all in this together, just on different pages, some that will meet and some that won't. My love for fairytales and for a happily ever after—which can mean different things to different people as one's way to fulfillment may not make sense to another—is why she who has evil associated with her name deserves her own story, her own side to things. Just like us all, she just wants to live, not be labelled as evil and have that define her path. She desires to make her own path and although she makes her fair share of mistakes, it all happens for a reason and we can learn from her resilience.

I would like to thank my wonderful ARC readers as well as my author and writer friends from Instagram that have made this experience all the more worthwhile with their support, encouragement and kind words that have meant more than they know. A special thanks goes out to my friends who have supported me since I began writing, some that provided me with suggestions and believed in my writing even when I doubted myself at times.

Most of all I want to thank my terrific parents and younger sister, Olivia for constantly having my back and being beyond supportive every step of the way. Thank you, mom, for teaching me to look at the bright side of things. That's what keeps me going when times feel tough, irritating or almost impossible. With this idea alone, it'll always feel as if you're guiding me through the situation as I'm undergoing it. This is a huge message in this book that allows the main character to understand that there's much more to life than surviving obstacles. She just must pass them first to have all the tools she needs to truly live, be happy and obtain the fulfillment she's always been after. Thank you, dad, for teaching me that people have a habit of testing our limits. We must know our values and worth to not fall into the trap of being a part of their world when it should be the other way around. This idea alone not only is a constant theme in this novel but is also something I highly believe in and has helped me a lot in real life. Thank you, Olivia, for not telling me to shut up during my constant book rants. Not to mention, you taught me that people aren't meant to be chased. Those that are meant to be in your life will find a way back into it even if you part ways. This is one of the themes in this novel and one of my key beliefs in my own life. These are all important life lessons that I have incorporated into my life and this book in particular which I love and can't help but agree with. None of this could've been possible without you and the support, encouragement, and motivation you provided me with. I am entirely grateful, thank you.

Contents

A Story to Live By	1
The Prophecy of Death	15
The Man in the Mirror	26
The Killer Pirate	39
The Game	52
The Freeing Blueprint	74
The Baby Project	88
The Disturbing News	101
Someone To Understand Me	111
Monsters Don't Get Love	123
Another Marble	139
Soulless	156
The Villain in His Story	169
The Constant Visitor	177
Freedom In A Mirror	184
About the Author	*203*

A Story to Live By

Live spelled backwards is evil. I didn't start out this way, was only trying my hardest to get by and not be the one always in pain for a change.

When people see good, there are expectations. I was once good and would say I still am. But one might argue in saying that being a princess with no blood on her hands and skin as white as snow is good. However being a queen who thought she committed two murders in one day for the sake of vengeance is malicious.

I do have a conscience, feel a burden for what I did. However, one single stab in the heart is nothing compared to the pain those two inflicted on me.

But nobody sees that. They see you as a villain and nothing else. Those that don't likely aren't aware of what you've done. You have to worry about them later seeing you as liar and therefore can't get too close.

Happy endings don't exist for those seen as villains but nobody cares to describe our lives, the truth of them all. The stories to showcase them throw us in the background as we destroy the person's life who destroyed ours. This is due to the real story being hidden from royalty since they'd never believe it coming from someone who married into that family. There is also the fact that some might view it as boring or taboo.

But whoever stumbles upon this story when the truth eventually comes out and will be believed is the judge of that. This is my story for those that need to hear that villains aren't villains but people who weren't treated with the respect they deserve. We maybe have made some poor decisions to make up for it that aren't necessarily our lifestyle or define us.

This story is called *Shattered* because it didn't start with the girl with snow white skin or an apple but a mirror, more in particular a man in it.

The evil queen is typically shown in a dark dress to compliment her dark hair and dark eyes but there once was light in me.

I was born with blonde hair that easily could've been mistaken for white and my eyes were a pale green but age and Chance changed that for me.

I grew up in a village across from the palace, a village called, Edgebrook. I'm not sure who named it but anyone that lived there was barely getting by. We all were on the edge, so the name suited it. Not to mention, the land looked ancient since no grass would grow on it for reasons unknown.

It wasn't a bad lifestyle though, allowed me to appreciate the little things that made our grassless land beautiful. I didn't take anything for granted since a simple task such as washing the laundry was done in the river which was time consuming and wasn't a thing in the winter. The schooling wasn't very advanced but was good enough and it was rare we didn't beg those who were less poor than us for food. It wasn't great but the less one has, the more there is to fill with adventure.

My mom passed when I was born since she wasn't wealthy enough to have me at a hospital or have a mid-wife in our hut instead of having my aunt Flora help deliver me. My aunt says it was due to the infection and pain she experienced during labor. As for my dad, he was hit by a truck on his way to work at the shoe factory. We're in the 21st century but villages near castles or royalty of any sort still go by the fact that men can only support the household outside of the house.

My aunt Flora raised me alongside her wife, Dedra, who I also viewed as my aunt and motherly figure even though they didn't marry until I was six. Aunt Flora is ten years older than my mom, so 35 at the time of my birth, and had been with Dedra since the two of them were 16. It was difficult for them to be together with the pressure of their parents to marry well to not struggle. Their parents weren't even against same sex marriage, it was the fact that they would barely be getting by since women only took care of the house, gathered berries and herbs and on occasion, watched other people's children to obtain little profit when they had no children of their own.

They eventually told their parents that they'd be willing to hardly get by in life because not living a full life together took their purpose away and promised they wouldn't bring any children into it. The pressure they felt and how poor they were was no life they desired for a child to live.

They didn't think my mom's husband would pass away, leaving her with not much more than them to get by off of or that they would be raising me when she passed. My aunt Flora assisted in the birth as she desired to be a nurse but wasn't allowed. As she took part in this, my aunt Dedra began to decorate the last several parts of my nursery my mom didn't get to with the grief she was facing due to my dad's passing a few weeks before her due date.

When I was a little girl, they would tell me that I was their blessing in disguise because I was a good thing that came out of a bad event. This was something they would've not considered having in their life if it wasn't for what took place.

My aunt Flora would say in her low, sweet and caring voice, "One look into your light spring eyes made me smile for my sister who barely saw you, but had a good enough glance to know you were beautiful. Your mama saw something in your aunt Dedra and me that we didn't when she muttered her love for you and love for us and how it makes sense for us to raise you. I couldn't answer her but your aunt rushed in the room and said yes for us immediately without even thinking because part of the reason we took so long to get married was that she wanted a child of her own, something we knew wouldn't be right for us to raise. She eventually came to an agreement because what I said made sense logically but she had hope in us I lacked. Even your mom didn't leave until I agreed too and as hard as I thought it would be, I loved every second of it."

She would say things like that when I felt purposeless when those at school looked down on me because the rags I used to wear proudly weren't good enough in the eyes of others. This resulted in much bullying that made me not want to go to school but my aunt Dedra would always tell me that life is hard. Even if I don't go to school, I'd know even less which wouldn't make life any easier and love is what makes it worth it.

Unfortunately, I eventually began to ignore what my classmates said and stand up for myself as well as make a friend who stayed close to me during laughs and cries, even in high school. This lead to me being chosen to have what was referred to as a better life, and saying no wasn't an option.

I was pulled out of my grade ten Science class early that day without an explanation until the principal brought me to his massive office as he was one of the few teachers in that school who clearly was well off. He instructed for me to take a seat behind his wooden desk that was freshly polished and sanded down. Beside the older man were my aunts with their long, tangled hair similar to my own and eyes full of love and concern.

"What's this about? Am I in trouble? Because this makes no sense when I am a good student, follow everything the teachers say and don't fight back when I'm picked on. I try to be the bigger person like my aunts have taught me," I defended myself and my aunt Dedra faintly smiled at my remark while my aunt Flora was trying her best not to cry.

"The king's wife passed away due to a sudden illness recently and he wants a young and healthy wife and mother for his three-year-old daughter, Sophia. It's a common occurrence for those with your status to be monitored since birth so an occurrence such as this can be a better life for someone like yourself. The king has been monitoring you since you were a little girl and is ready for you to be his wife," the principal explained to me in a stern tone of voice, barely fazed by his statement that involved a 15-year-old girl to marry the king who was a little less than twice her age, 28. I focused on his sky-blue dress shirt with white buttons in misery as I had nothing to say and desired for the colours to blur and be a nightmare then and there. Yet that was anything but the case.

"Her parents are dead and she is being raised by a lesbian couple! We even named her after her dead mother for Christ's sake, Viola. Why does he want her? There are so many other girls who are better off, don't have their hair in knots or a dirty smile and some of these girls are also in this village, in the same class," my aunt Dedra attempted to use her rough voice and bluntness to change the principal's mind but it wasn't his decision. This was all while my aunt Flora was lost in words as she didn't want a child with Dedra and now, she couldn't picture herself without one.

"He wants her because of the prophecy of the apple. Your niece was born with a birthmark in the shape of an apple on her right shoulder. There are three girls like her, the first was his wife, then her and even his daughter, Sophia, has the same marking. If you look at the bible, an apple refers to temptation and original sin, what began our world and that is what is needed for a strong kingdom this king will create. With temptation and original sin also come wisdom and possibly love, health and happiness when learned from. I was instructed to get both you and your wife's signatures to ensure the marriage can be official and if I don't, I was paid to kill you both and take her anyway, so the choice is yours," the principal I suddenly feared explained and my aunt Flora's wrinkles from stress were more visible ok her forehead as shook her head with the knowledge that this was no better life and wouldn't sign to that. My aunt Dedra shrieked every curse word that weren't looked well upon when coming from a woman's mouth while she tore out some of her fiery red strands of straight, tangled hair. "Drink some water, breathe and calm down before you sign anything," he reassured them and handed them two cups of water from the back they both took small sips of as my aunt Flora was breathing in and out to soothe herself and reassured me everything would be okay while my aunt Dedra told me we'd find a way out of this. However, I wasn't at all reassured when I too asked for water and he refused.

"Your water was poisoned! Don't drink anymore!" I shouted in worry, but my aunts trusted him too easily due to their concern for me.

"Be yourself and you'll be alright. Love you, my darling," my aunt Flora responded weakly before her light spring eyes shut forever on the other side of the desk.

"Have fun in luxury to make the best out of it and we'll always be with you," my aunt Dedra added, slurring her words before she blew me a kiss I caught and placed it on my heart before she passed out forever.

"The king is a very nice man and knows you will make as much of a great influence his first wife did when she was queen," the principal added as I focused on the faces of my aunts that looked peaceful, not mentally drained for the first time in all I've known them before I followed the principal to the back door of his office he gestured towards, not bothering to argue for obvious reasons.

Before I followed him, I kissed both of my aunts on the cheeks as I held their ice cold hands briefly as I said a quick farewell. I followed the principal into what appeared to be a supply closet yet was anything but that with the fancy, middle-aged woman in the navy pantsuit and racks of clothes as well as every hair product and removal imaginable.

"Viola, I shall prepare you for the day you will forever treasure and bring you by carriage to the palace for the ceremony in two hours," The blush haired woman with a British accent explained and I nodded, all I had the strength to do as she pulled my body every direction in her attempt to make me artificially beautiful. "If you don't try to escape the castle until you are of legal age, your aunts will be fine. They aren't dead, were just given a drug to make them appear that way and will wake up to being told to pretend they never raised you unless they want harm put upon you," she added, slightly relieving me.

"I won't leave then," I mumbled as she closed and locked the door behind us, about to start a torturous process.

I still don't know to this day how she managed to make me look so unlike myself, so clean in only a storage closet with a sink with a hose. My ragged clothes and undergarments were torn off me with the strong woman's bare hands, leaving me standing there stark naked as she basically used the sink hose to give me a shower without any curtains. I stood there, my body practically numb in discomfort and humiliation as she washed every inch of me with vanilla scented soap.

Much dirt was left as residue on the cold, hard beige floor since the soap we'd manage to make wasn't all that great but she didn't look down on that or down on my body that was full of hair that wasn't too noticeable since my hair is light. She didn't even hand me a towel next, instead plugged in a blow drier into an empty outlet. I've only heard of a blow drier and never used one. The special one she had allowed every hair of mine to blow both directions and then be dry. She continued on by waxing every area I had with hair, including touching up my eyebrows. She obviously didn't wax the hair on my head which felt as if it was practically pulled out of my scalp as it was being untangled in a rough, quick and efficient manner with another hair tool that only royalty possessed.

By the end of it all, I wasn't only in pain but red all over from the amount of waxing and pulling that took place. I was patted down with smudge proof and water proof makeup to hide it all until the redness left. After, I was given fancy, white undergarments with lace and real diamonds along the edges to put on which I did as I admired them in surprise that something so nice could be put on someone who was usually covered in dirt if not treated like it.

In my undergarments, did the woman who looked to be in her late 30s or early 40s, put a special gold comb through my hair that had my tangled curls, appear like ringlets. She even added some rose water to my face as well as some light peach lipstick.

"Most royalty wear corsets, but you, my lady, are what some call royally thin, so we have a few layers we'll be placing under your dress that aren't attached to it, to make you not look like you've been starved to death and make it look like you actually have your menstrual cycle and therefore have breasts and hips," she voiced her insensitive opinion as she put a layer on top of my bra to lift my breasts up even more and practically suffocate them, along with a similar tight, light peach colour material to match my skin tone and hug my hips before she threw a white dress of many layers over my head.

I closed my eyes while she patted all of the layers down inside and out as I was afraid an inner layer with sequence would blind me. The woman then proceeded by zipping me up in the back, placing a silver necklace with an apple charm composed of expensive gems on my neck and apple red heels to match it.

"I can't walk in these and this dress is stuffy and hot!" I whined to her as I looked at the long, lacy sleeves of the dress that looked as if it could've been a table cloth in an elderly woman's home as I almost fell until the blush haired woman pulled me back up.

"Be happy that's all you'll be complaining about. You're lucky this king has morals and is fine with no physical intimacy until the age of 18. By then you're an adult and by then all foretold in the prophecy will be brought to the kingdom by you. That age is also the age you can choose to stay or go because then the marriage will be completely legal if you redo it that year, not a grey area. You'll have your own bedroom, own responsibilities and experiences…"

"I want to see my room before the wedding," I whimpered in my attempt to show little weakness as I concealed my tears.

"You want to see what's left of you because you can't see yourself in a mirror right now and want to see how good something that belongs to you is unlike everything else. I know how hard it is, that's why I tried to be quick and rough with you because if I showed I cared, too many people would get hurt. It's best I stay out but my daughter, Gloria, will be your personal assistant and if you're ever lonely enough to hear my story, just ask her or ask for her mother, Mrs. O'Neil. I don't have the title of Lady like my daughter. She is a personal assistant by choice but duchess by love. I would say marriage but she isn't very practical. Her children have her boyfriend's last name before her," Mrs. O'Neil made me feel a sense of comfort through how she related and how I'd be assisted by her daughter. It was her rambling that caught me off guard due to the nerves of it all. I nodded respectfully while she pulled out a wand she claimed to borrow from one of the palace fairies but it didn't matter because it got me there in my room without being seen or so I thought.

"You're not as trapped as you think you are. Have fun with what you're given, make it a wedding nobody will forget for very bad reasons," a male voice that was rebellious yet had much depth to it with its soft tone that sounded young and lost, stated as soon as I entered the room without Mrs. O'Neil.

"I'm not going to act like a child because this wedding will happen games or not even if I can barely recognize myself," I voiced glumly to the girl in the large, rectangular mirror across from my bed with the lavender coloured silk comforter and sheets.

I studied her artificial curls, glossed lips, waxed legs in pointy shoes I've seen but never wore due to my status in society and the white, long-sleeved dress full of excess lace, even around the turtle neck collar.

"That's not beauty! That's ridiculous!" the same voice from before said what I was thinking before I could.

"Who are you because my conscience doesn't sound like that?" I asked in utter fear that worse was ahead of me.

"Chance and I'll show myself to you when I think you're ready to understand why you have a man in the mirror," he intrigued me by his statement alone.

"Why do I have a man in my mirror?" I asked him in disbelief.

"You'll love me enough to have it in you to kill me," he paused for dramatic effect. "Now, I think that's enough for today," he taunted me with his dangerous words that had me throw a white marble chair at the mirror which laid across from the desk in my room. The mirror however didn't break, only the chair and my bedroom door busted open at the ruckus alone. "Only your love for me can break this mirror, no object," he whispered so only I could hear.

"Chad, leave her alone!" A handsome man who looked around ten years older than myself, with a deep voice, sharp jawline and mid-length, silky, chocolate brown hair that was combed back, had my attention.

"I thought this turd's name was Chance," I responded in annoyance as I allowed my eyes to roll.

"He wants people to see him differently, take a chance on him but he's Chad. He'll always be Chad because his ways don't change no matter how he is with you. I'm warning you that all he makes you feel has been felt before with women before you that didn't give into the manipulation. If they did, he'd be standing out here with us instead of inside of a mirror. Trust me when I say he'll use the same tricks on you he did with my first wife, Melana," the charming man who smirked at my name for Chance, revealed himself to be my soon to be husband.

His warning unfortunately didn't do me good for very long. In reality, I closed my white door shut as soon as I entered the bedroom which was later in the day and began to play games with the devil in sheep's clothing.

Today I can still say I see him as Chance because change he did but the change didn't last very long. When I realized that was why he didn't deserve to live, I killed her because I killed him. That's what nobody addresses and why my story, our story is framed in such a way that it shows her forcing irons on my feet to dance to my death because in a bystander's eyes, she is worth rooting for, not the other way around.

The Prophecy of Death

"It's not even a real ceremony. We're just standing by an alter in a church and getting photographs of the big day because either way, it isn't legal until you decide to continue your legacy here on your own since your legal guardians signed nothing. There's no need to be afraid and if this narcissist that thinks his name is Chance is bothering you, I'll cover up all the mirrors and put gloss on it that blurs out his speech to your ears," The king reassured me with his kind words and welcoming, English accent that separated those with status and those without.

"I think I can handle a weasel and thank you for everything," I voiced to him kindly as I glared at his fancy white suit.

"His suit is classy but you won't stand a chance in his world, don't belong in it," Chance mocked me once again, but I showed him by removing the loose, long sleeves from my arms and tying them in a small bow for the back of the dress.

"You're right," I stated with a smile, a genuine one, not one full of hatred, frustration or annoyance. He told me the truth, understood me and knew what was real. There was so much more to him yet that was all I noticed at the time, all I felt the need of knowing, him.

"The dress was traditional but took away from your youth and I know it will photograph well," the king added as he put his hand in my own, forgetting about the carriage entrance because through my act of tying the sleeves to make a bow at the back of my dress, he instantly knew a change had to be made with how humble royals were.

I remember that day as if it were yesterday because it was a day I felt purpose for the first time in my life. It wasn't walking along the floors with the fancy, shiny tiles or being so close to a man I barely knew when we pretended to kiss during our fake ceremony or even the tiara that was placed on my head when I was crowned queen. It was the little girl that watched the entire thing in the front row of the dining hall.

She was the only one that was there along with photographers. This palace wasn't like most in England where it would be crowded during massive events, where outsiders knew everything about everyone there and it only dictated a nearby village. It wasn't given a lot of power, just enough. The only reason it existed was because a poor village with not too much around it or to live off of had nothing to compare itself to, didn't even think of itself as poor until people with a smarter, more industrialized and wealthy way of living decided it was meant to be controlled.

One look into the little girl's large, sapphire blue eyes that were on her small, round, snow white face, told me I belonged in this palace for her. I was chosen so the little girl with the blush coloured bow over her head, the girl in the puffy, blush coloured dress with the round, massive, short sleeves that were covered in daisies along with the long dress with the rectangular-shaped neckline, could be more than a princess alone.

I desired for her to be more than one in a fancy outfit with an adorable face of natural beauty and stunning smile just as I desired for myself to be more than the girl in rags. Beauty exceeds sight. Beauty is meant to be felt and I wanted to show her that through small acts by not wearing my tiara because I wasn't above anyone in the palace and befriending anyone who appeared approachable, birds included that had the habit of sitting on the windowsill of my bedroom.

"Can she stand up here with us, king?" I asked the king I still didn't know the name of, who was going to be my "husband" while staring at the phony minister in front of us and then the large room with colourful banners on the walls I didn't understand.

"You can call me Liam, my queen, and that is a splendid idea…"

"First kiss me!" I interrupted him, giving into the immediate physical attraction and how close we were during the pretend kiss.

"I thought it looked realistic enough seconds before but you are beautiful and will be a big part of my life, so I don't see why…"

It was then that I lessened the distance completely, unaware of if I kissed him correctly, if there was a correct way of kissing as it was only my first time. It was a strange thing though because correct or not, there was something between us that made it difficult to pull apart in that moment.

"I think that was more real than people expected," he added as he parted from our intimate moment.

"Was I that bad?" I asked him I concern.

"No, a bad kiss doesn't linger for that long. My wife hasn't passed long enough for something like that to feel appropriate but who am I to judge," he added coyly as he went in for seconds, practically tackling me on the golden palace tiles we were standing on, allowing his body to press against my own as he pushed his weight against me, allowing me to feel an unexpected warmth I wasn't used to. He was still a gentleman though, didn't push his luck, didn't tug at my dress or kiss me anywhere other than my lips and he didn't keep me on the floor very long. He soon grabbed my hand to lift me up, threw a handsome smile my direction and invited his daughter, Sophia, to join us up front as I suggested.

"This woman here is going to be a very special part of our lives. She isn't your mom but will look after us both like your mom wished she had done here. You can call her qu..."

"Viola is more than okay and we have many changes to make here that will make your mom proud. One, being that women can get jobs and provide in the village because women deserve independence that other parts of England and this palace have. The village needs to be more modern and be given the needed transportation to leave it and leave the country if one wants to explore or move elsewhere and nobody in the village wants it shoved in their faces that there is a better way of living, how poor we really are. Not only do royals need to be more modest and seem more humane by making some personal things about them such as their names public but to share the wealth and not just collect money from the poor but give money to them. This dress looks expensive that I'm wearing, extravagant clothing items or unnecessary event costs can be cut a little so the poor can live a bit more comfortably," I crouched in front of the little girl to be more approachable as I gazed into her curious sapphire blue eyes and then her dad's that looked like the clouded version of hers.

"We can start by making the village more modern and go from there but things like this take time, can't be done in a day and have to be announced publicly. Since you think our public appearance isn't so modest or comforting, you're going to speak with us," he agreed and didn't suggest the second part, more so told me what to do which irritated me.

"Thank you but if this is going to work, me bringing whatever was told I'd bring to your kingdom, I ask of you to please ask me my duties, not tell me them because even with my aunt's lives and peace on the line, I don't belong to you or anyone. I'm not property but a person with feelings like everyone else," I voiced to him and just as he acknowledged my suggestion with a nod, did his little girl answer for him.

"Good idea and can you please no kiss again. That was what he done with mommy," Sophia asked, speaking quite well for the age of three and I listened to her request as Liam did with mine.

We agreed to have an admirable friendship, leaving that make out session behind us and being positive role models in Sophia's life in a way that didn't terrify her. We were both open to the idea of something more than friends in the future but that was to think about when I could legally marry him and when Sophia understood that I was by no means replacing her mom.

However, I knew I'd never fully get involved with the king physically or emotionally because he was anything but a gentleman. I didn't try to escape before I turned 18 to ensure my aunts were safe and because then I'd have nobody.

I felt trapped in my own home and had Chance to thank for that but he did make me feel safe and understood when the sun was asleep and the moon was glistening. That was the only time we were ever truly alone.

I believed the king's promises and honesty until he told me to get changed for dinner one evening. He offered for my personal assistant to help me but I wanted a little time with Chance, felt everything was a little too perfect to be true. I told Liam that I wanted a half hour to myself which he seemed to believe.

I remember sitting against my door and asking Chance to speak but things were never that simple with him.

"About what? I still don't think you're ready to see me, so you won't until I say so if that's what this is about!" he annoyed me with his assumption of me.

"You don't decide that for me but that is beyond the point! Why don't you think I belong here?

Why do you feel the need to taunt me with your words?" I asked him in wonder, my back against the door and my arms crossed.

"There are mirrors in every inch of this place including the main hall, so tell me why did you kiss him out of lust and not want to see any more of that for a while because of the girl? That girl will be what makes you leave here when you're beginning to think of it as a home," he perplexed me with his words as he had a habit of doing.

"You can't say things like this I don't understand!" I shouted, aggravated at the large mirror in the distance.

This triggered him to show me what no 15-year-old girl needed to see. The mirror fogged to show a younger version of the king, when he was only a teenager. His mid-length, coffee brown hair was parted to the side instead of the middle and he was wearing a fancy, sky-blue jacket with black dress pants as his father handed him a sand coloured scroll he unrolled to inform the young prince of his future.

This castle is in great doom with the way things are run. There must be some changes put in place for it to be a part of the future. You, my king, aren't capable of putting them in place because you will die after reading this but your son is, will unite three with apple markings on their right shoulder. The first he finds, will be his true love. Her purpose is to help your son understand happiness and love in ways he never had before until he gets bored of her since she hadn't changed the kingdom besides blessing him with a daughter. He will poison her slowly with powders hidden in her meal that will make it appear as if she passed from a sudden illness. His daughter with the apple marking will have beauty that is a weapon but when put in the right hands will make the kingdom strong and his second wife will not only add a modern take to life in Edgebrook but will find a way to showcase her voice for the greater good even if his daughter is the death of her.

Chance continued by fading out the scroll and showing me the plain mirror. "I can't be close to either one of them, can I?"

"No, but you can be close to me," he stated in a way that almost sounded like begging, but I didn't give in or feel anything for him.

"Why would I want to do that?" I replied with much sass present in my voice while he allowed me to see much more than my own reflection in the mirror but what lied in it.

He revealed his beige coloured face and chest to me, highlighting his lines of all lengths and angles that acted as permanent scars of his life before the mirror. "Because you know what it's like to be taken away from those you love with the prophecy of your death from someone you already care so much about. You know what it's like to feel cut, wounded and know that being alone, feeling empty or confined in a large space won't do your burdens any good," he sighed. "I wasn't a good man before this but making me a way nobody could ever love to feel like I broke so many girls is cruel. I may have broke them but someone can still love a girl with a broken heart that needs a little tending, not a boy who can't leave the mirror unless he wants to crack just like it. I'm alone in here, my body bare, every inch cracked, including what a woman expects to eventually please her in the act of love making," Chance looked down, his dirty blonde hair that landed around his ears was messy unlike the king's and his sapphire green eyes to compliment my light spring eyes, grew dark.

I felt terrible for him as he looked like puzzle pieces with his entire body being scarred, taking away from his toned arms, abs, chocolate chip-like nipples and round face to focus on his sharp features. He blurred out his parts under his waist for obvious reasons yet already exposed so much to me.

"You clearly treated women like objects, you'd toss away and move on to the next when you lost interest. So, someone that I have a feeling I'd get along with well, put you in here and you need to not feel empty like they have because of you to get out and feel free?" I mocked him. "You were put in mirrors of a palace that isn't that well-known so nobody can save you in a place full of snobs and I can't save you either. Even me hypothetically loving you enough to kill you won't do you any good because what those women were missing was a healthy relationship within themselves. Look beneath the cracks and you can break your own curse, and close your eyes while I change," I suggested and asked of him as I moved away from the door to change out of my uncomfortable dress I untied, undid the back of and lifted up and over my head which I laid on my bed.

"You do have an assistant you know," he teased me, clearly ignoring when I told him to close his eyes.

"And you don't always need everything you have right away. Now cover your eyes, you perv!" I exclaimed in utter frustration.

"And miss out on seeing your naked body?" he joked at my nude coloured undergarments to shape my body to appear more mature looking.

"You're so immature," I rolled my eyes at him. "I might have had a weird idea about romantic love, about being made fun of my entire life being worth it because he'd make me feel comforted in a way that even if we didn't see eye to eye on everything, he would look at things from my perspective to make me feel less helpless and guide me where he could, treat it as our problem instead of mine. My aunts who raised me have that and you get to high school and eventually think that you're all you got. I had one close friend that was always there for me but knew that wouldn't last forever because that was my luck with things and I was right when I was separated from her and was brought here. I went for a kiss with Liam so I can say that I know what it's like to be kissed if we never do become more than friends. The closeness encouraged it but it was still my decision. I don't love him and he doesn't love me but I love me and that's what is keeping me going, that and my aunts who showed me that no love is forbidden or easy to give up on when it means something," I proved a point I used to feel insecure about until I met Chance.

He didn't say anything as a response, just put his right hand up to the glass as he waited for my hand to meet his and I slowly approached him to do just that which became our daily thing every time we woke up or went to bed to tell each other we'd never be alone.

"Okay, I'll try what you're saying but only if we can talk more tonight, doll face," Chance attempted to compromise and called me a nickname that would have most girls feeling warm and fuzzy all over but by the nickname, I knew he ignored my advice.

"Sure, whatever you want, doll ass," I replied harshly, knowing things were anything but done between us.

I was always the type to want to help when no one else would or could. Yet to help and not have him take my help, let me keep my distance and tune him out. It encouraged me to befriend my personal assistant who helped me out in more ways than just informing me of palace activities and assisting me in changing my outfits and styling my hair. If he took my help right away, I know I wouldn't be standing where I am today, outside of the palace or Edgebrook with a new take on life with a fresh mirror I only plan to see myself through.

The Man in the Mirror

Over the course of a year, I made a difference in the palace but didn't have myself feeling too comfortable with the prophecy that Sophia would be the end of me. There were only two people I felt completely myself in front of, Chance and Gloria.

Gloria didn't only become my personal assistant but became my best friend. She later saw much more of me than she would've liked since Chance and I got really close and a mirror between us didn't stop us from doing things most couples would do to express themselves to each other. That didn't happen until I was 16 however, the age Chance was trapped in the mirror at and stayed, although we did get close in other ways before that.

We'd spend nights sleeping beside one another, the mirror separating us yet I felt as if I could feel him and that had nothing to do with the blanket I'd lie in curled up in a ball next to him.

Most nights, I wouldn't even sleep until it was too late and it would mess me up for the day following it.

We'd share conversations like none other that made me not see it worth as closing my eyes for even a second until I felt the need to. It wouldn't be one's typical discussion but deep things, like how stars manage to stand out in the dark sky when they are bright but so small.

"Thanks for leaving me alone to know I too can love my cracks but don't ever leave me again. I ask this of you, not tell you, Viola," he voiced to me desperately the first night I spent at the palace and said I was too far from him when I slept in the most comfortable bed that was much more than an old mattress with its springs hanging on for dear life. That was the night I began to sleep by the mirror in my long, turquoise coloured nightgown I was provided with but detested with how easy it was to trip over and how hot it made me at night.

"It's your home too. Try going to bed feeling like yourself. I can see all through this mirror and have seen glimpses of you when I was meant to and you don't wear this to bed in Edgebrook," he would speak about me in ways that suggested he knew me better than I knew myself.

"There isn't anything here to wear that is similar to that," I explained and he chuckled, amused by his imagination

"I'm wearing something to bed so don't you get all turned on!" I shouted at him, slightly laughing as I'd likely be more comfortable bare than in the tight undergarments, itchy and long nightgown, but not in front of him. That would've only taught him to act as he did before the mirror, in the mirror.

"Fine but what about what goes under the dress? There has to be something more comfortable there," he suggested and I shook my head as I rummaged through the massive closet, feeling every material there was and feeling like Chance's idea was looking better and better until I thought I found another set of sheets tucked in the closet that weren't silk like the plum coloured ones on my bed that felt foreign. It however was a plain white pillow that was a small square and looked to be for a chair but was likely thrown in there due to its simplicity. I instantly grabbed the pillow and striped down in the back of the mirrorless closet so Chance couldn't see me. I then tied a thin, black piece of fabric to myself that must've been put in there by accident. This was to have the pillow stay attached to the front of me, landing at my hips, covering all it needed to.

There wasn't a second pillow, meaning my back wasn't covered but most people's backs and cracks looked similar, so I wasn't too concerned if he saw that.

"Before you ask, the bedding feels weird, even the blanket on the edge and it's summer, so I shouldn't catch a cold and this is the best I think I can do," I admitted to him as he erased my face and body in the mirror briefly to make it look like my outfit was on him to put a smile on his face until he blurred his bottom half as he always had.

"You were right about why I was put in here and it was a queen herself that did this to me, Melana. We had a thing going on before she was chosen by the king. It wasn't anything special to me. She was just another number, but it was everything to her. She knew what kind of guy I was and knew she was only what I did on weekends but she began to care for me and instead of letting me let her go, she had the king trap me in here to learn from my mistakes in a place where there are too many snobs and so much backtalk about me," he confessed as I placed my hand on his yet again to tell him that it was okay.

"The queen didn't know about me, well I'm sure she did but I mean that I'd be here for you. Focus on the love she only imagined from you, never felt, feel strong and happy when I can't be here with you and when I can, be vulnerable like now. I like seeing you like this, like a human, not the monster people painted you out to be," I replied to him honestly.

"Okay, I treated women like numbers because that's all I was as a boy. I was in a foster home and the older I got, people would put me further and further down the list when they'd mention the children they had to adopt. My older brother was adopted at a young age and I hardly ever see him but that's luck for you," he slightly paused for reflection. "Uh, I eventually left at 16 because there was one house that wanted me when I was 13 but immediately returned me when I fell in love with their daughter who died of cancer and her parents had too much to grieve over since she was an only child and didn't think they were in the right mindset to raise a 14-year-old boy. Then, I went through the motions during my days and eventually left the foster home, ran away and relied on hookups to keep me happy since I couldn't believe in love since what happened to Lucy. Those hookups gave me a place to stay that night and well, you know how the rest goes," he opened up to me as my bedroom door opened with a ticked off Gloria with a cranky Rosalyn in her arms.

Gloria was admirable. She was practically a single mom in her late teens as she was a little less than three years older than myself. Her daughter was barely eight months and she was already a few months pregnant with baby number two. Like her mother mentioned, she wasn't married but she did have a boyfriend who was in the royal military and around this time, there was a dangerous battle for our castle to potentially expand and become more well-known, something nearby villages were against. They had been fighting hard and she didn't know when she'd see him next. He knew about their second child on the way through the letters they'd exchange.

Her soot black hair was done up in curlers, her golden skin was covered in what looked to be a sparkly blue face scrub and she was in a long, rose coloured nightgown with lace along the U-neck trim and spaghetti straps, a similar design to my uncomfortable nightgown.

"What are you wearing; you do know the mirror boy can see you and not just hear you, and what happened to sleeping in your bed?" she questioned me in her Spanish accent that was intimidating and sounded nothing like her mother's English accent as she was adopted. She whispered me her concerns as she attempted to calm her daughter that was her carbon copy in her arms as she whispered lullabies in her ears.

"Nothing is comfortable besides this pillow. Even the fancy undergarments hurt!" I complained and she placed her daughter on the silky pillow on my bed she removed the case of, making her her own bed while she wrapped her in the pillow case, soothing her instantly as she focused her attention on me.

"Okay, I do have more comfortable fabrics I can customize your clothes from, just ask next time, especially if you sort of share a room with a boy. Chance, please watch my little Rosa for a few minutes while I make Viola something more suitable to sleep in," she instructed him and he listened without giving her any attitude or saying anything dirty. "I've made more comfortable and modern stuff I have in a little box in the back. It's all a size small and should fit you. If not, it'll do for tonight and we'll make more tomorrow," she said kindly as she pulled me out a cement grey sport's bra and matching cotton underwear as well as a cotton nightgown that didn't itch or drag and was the colour peach.

I put the ensemble on in the back of the closet and thanked her as I felt more comfortable and closer to my real home than I did in the long nightgown.

She handed me a soft blanket that was slightly piling to ensure I'd be warm on the floor and gave me the pillow I used as an outfit as well.

"Thanks," I said graciously.

"No worries but don't tell this guy too much because you need to remember that it's not only you he sees and talks to in the mirrors. There are other girls in the palace," she warned.

"Nobody this deep," I said defensively, crossing my arms while Gloria brushed them down and placed them along my sides.

"You just met him, so be cautious," she looked out for me but annoyed me in the process.

"I know what I'm doing but thanks, mom," I mocked her and she did continue to look out for me until she betrayed me like everyone before her had.

I may have never grown up with my mom but felt enough love at home from my two parental figures. Aunt Flora always knew the right things to say and aunt Dedra knew the right things to do based on logic and feeling. They balanced each other out and made me feel complete. Gloria was my home away from home as she protected me in ways only they were capable of and I saw her as my best friend at the time for that.

That night, I slept by the mirror for a few hours and chatted during the rest. My throat felt utterly sore and bitter in the morning but felt worth it at the time.

I dreaded leaving my room at the palace and that had nothing to deal with me being sleep deprived. It did however have everything to do with me feeling as if I missed a part of myself when I was with my apparent husband or was spending the day being poked at as outfits were being customized on me. I was required to attend the palace spa at least once a week to look my best self and could never fully relax.

A part of me would always be tense because thinking of someone one couldn't say much about without getting hurt was nowhere close to being with them. I did come up with the solution of bringing a compact mirror wherever I went, constantly pretending to be full of myself and my appearance to even just catch a quick gaze of his sapphire green beauties.

It's a complete misconception when people hear about the "evil" queen constantly asking the mirror who the fairest, most stunning woman is and being disappointed and vengeful when she no longer heard her name. The truth is that she would smile at what those assumed was herself until nobody was in the mirror, following her every move, which made her sad.

She questioned him and when he felt smothered, she stopped carrying that mirror around. She began to feel his presence in other ways by hearing his voice and thoughts wherever she went in her own because that's how close they were and she assumed he did the same for her.

The older she got, the more of herself she gave to him. First, her mind, body and lastly, the hardest of all, heart.

Sentiments shared at night that ranged from thoughts behind aspects of scenery, to questions about the world and its existence, the whole hierarchy in society to be more precise along with its expectations opened many doors. First an emotional need and later a physical need when a certain age was reached that came along with urges one would assume couldn't be met with a mirror between them but that was anything but true.

As time passed, the queen when close enough to the mirror could make love to the man without touching the glass, only him. They understood each other so much to the point that they couldn't feel the glass between them, only the warmth, curves, movement and loving embrace of one another.

It was when the girl was nearing the age of 18, looking more and more like a woman that she didn't need her curves or breasts enhanced by fabric, that things began to change with three special words.

"I love you! I want to be with you without limitations, without hiding us! I want you to rule with me not Liam who is a friend at most that is willing to give women independence but tax everyone in the village double. With you, we'd do good because you know what it's like to feel unheard, unseen and how people like us deserve leaders that will give them a good life," I voiced to him desperately the morning I realized all I offered Edgebrook wasn't enough. I was prohibited from visiting the village and was deceived about what was actually occurring with it until I heard a conversation between Liam and one of the tax workers.

"We've been together for around three years and you love me? I thought you were only comfortable with me?" he questioned me as I lessened the distance between us, knowing him well enough that he only wanted to whisper what he really thought in case anyone was listening. This would be because he didn't want to prove people wrong, only himself and he desired to love someone as much as himself when it appeared growing up nobody else did. Sadly that person was the girl he lost, his first love, a girl who wasn't me.

"I love you too, Sophia!" he didn't whisper it as he tended to whisper emotional and sexual thoughts about me. He shouted it, practically did from the roof tops. My door flew open as the mirror did what it wasn't capable of by human force and only emotion, love to be more exact. The mirror crashed, tiny specks that charged a mile a minute, hitting my flesh and causing it to bleed. But he didn't care, only cared about the girl I didn't notice behind me who was nearly seven. This was the girl who was foretold to be the end of me according to the prophecy yet whoever predicted what they did, didn't know more than the man who could see anything he desired through the mirrors, past, present and even future. People say very personal things in front of the mirror or even stare at themselves in ways nobody else would, ways someone behind the glass can know their entirety from.

"She's not even seven! You're 16, Chance since you don't age in the mirror, and you love me, shared personal stuff with me, like how you lost Lucy, how you found it hard to love yourself when it appeared nobody else did! You told me the truth when nobody else did; you said I couldn't survive here if I wasn't myself! You even made love to me! I did all I was capable of doing for Edgebrook, it isn't great but better and I'll find other ways to make it more than better or decent, but the best it can be! And by being myself I found someone who understands me and a best friend who designs more than my outfits but makes me feel like a queen when my voice isn't heard as much as it should be and looks out for me by comforting me when someone special to me, you, confuses me or seems to not be completely honest. So, if you always loved her and it wasn't me, tell me why so I don't wonder!" I ordered him sternly as I basically exposed him and embarrassed myself in front of Gloria, Liam and some of the palace help who were all crowded by the door when they heard the glass shatter. They noticed the bare man exit it without any scratches or scars on the broken body I gave so much love to.

"If you love me so much, you'll understand I needed you to feel something a child wouldn't understand yet. I see it in her eyes. She's Lucy in another form! Lucy found me and that's who I would watch and talk to when you weren't around. That's why I didn't want you to carry me around with you everywhere. I did fall for you but not in the way I fell for Lucy and will never stop loving her," he crushed me more and more with each and every word that made me feel trampled on, ignored, manipulated, as flesh didn't only bleed but my tears did too, leaving stains on my cheeks as I grabbed a large shard of glass and stabbed where his heart was. I went as far as carving a heart into the top left side of his chest.

I heard gasps behind me, and Liam pulled his daughter away from the situation while Gloria attempted to pull me back. I had enough force on Chance to not allow her to pull me back as I took a final stab in his heart, heard one final scream from Liam as Liam lost a daughter and Chance and Lucy could finally be together.

I stood still with blood on the tips of my fingers of the glass I dropped on the ground to witness shatter even further as Chance died with a smile on his face but not the little girl I treated like a sister when her dad wasn't able to look after her.

Her snow white skin lost its colour quickly while more bloodshot tears escaped my cheeks as I watched a decent man lose his only child as he sobbed over her tiny face.

"The servants rushed to get the police. We both lied to each other and didn't want this to happen. Run and take Gloria's papers with you. It's too dangerous to take her and her daughter with you because you might look different but if someone sees the blood, you're done," Liam sounded like a genuinely good ruler for the first time.

I faintly smiled despite my reflection I caught a glimpse of in the scattered pieces of glass on the floor. My blonde hair that was almost white, suddenly was jet black and when I brushed it out with my fingers, I lost half of my long, thick locks. It was instantly short and thin, and the blonde laid on the ground.

Even my eyes weren't pure, but hazel with a tint of orange, full of much darkness. Nothing was unique about them.

I muttered sorry to him as blood continued to drip down my face and I ran into Gloria's room for her to quickly help me clean up before my life changed.

Wealth has nothing to do with happiness but those you are surrounded with and love do. When you're taken away from those you love, your heart breaks a little and when betrayal enters it, it shatters so much that it can no longer be recognized. I couldn't recognize the woman that stared back at me who was by no means the naive girl that arrived at the palace, feeling homesick because she didn't understand that your home follows you in your heart.

My emotions took over me like heat in an oven cooking raw dough that was supposed to be bread. I was supposed to be dead but instead was known as evil.

The Killer Pirate

Gloria pulled my hand towards her room, that's how numb my body was. I wanted to be caught then and there, to scream out that I killed Sophia and the man in the mirror because I deserved to be punished.

But the more she pulled me, the more I began to realize that mistake or not, I wasn't asked to live in a castle. I wasn't asked to be deceived by two people and have my heart broken. By law I was guilty but by morals, emotions, I was innocent.

Yet do innocent people have a friend wash blood off them that isn't caused from wounds or glass that vanished as if it was never in my skin, some that temporarily stained me as birthmarks, dark, glum, blobs?

The blobs of red weren't exactly blobs as they formed an image close to my heart which resembled a heart composed of splatters of red on my left side where my heart is, by my lips and I even felt it drip along my pelvic region.

I was a complete freak. Nobody would ever love me and my lack of honesty would have nothing to do with it.

I was cleansed with a damp cloth of the blood that didn't make pictures on my body which Gloria managed to soak up. She then carried on by covering my visible marks in bronze cover-up, what had become of my pure, peach skin. She used her talented makeup skills to make it appear as if no red splatters ever laid near my lips or chest.

She then proceeded by handing me a suitcase full of everything I needed for the city, clearly having had prepared it far in advance.

"How?" were my only words to her, traumatized by the shock of my actions, numbing pain and change they provided me with.

"He'd sing her songs in the mirror, hoping she'd remember him but he was more broken than the mirror because he saw a child that looked similar to his Lucy and loved her like it was her, only had passion with you. The girl saw him as he saw her because he cared for her in a way nobody else had, so they shared one heart, the one existing outside of the mirror, hers. She wasn't smiling because he loves Lucy, not her, and she might be young but feels as in love and as broken as you are. I'm not your mom, didn't want to meddle, so I stood by the sidelines and prepared an escape plan if the prophecy flipped because it's been known to happen and I can't come with you but wanted to help as much as I could," she stated teary eyed and I hugged her ever so tightly, my cold self taking in her warmth but not so much that I would cry because we didn't have much more time to clean up any bloody tears.

"Thank you," I managed to mutter. "I wouldn't have survived here without your cotton fabric, kind heart, friendship and adorable children to play with," I faintly grinned as we parted from the embrace.

"You wouldn't survive in the nearest city either, Marchland, but you're now known as Violet instead of Viola, to still keep most of your mother's name. But you can't use your royal last name, Welington or your peasant last name, Marley. Your new last name is Grey, the G for Gloria, a little something to remember me by. Any potential document you need is in there and you weren't 18 when you wed, so you got no legal ties here. Just try not to wear anything white that people know was originally white because like the dress you're wearing that was once white, it'll turn black. And if you fall in love again, which you will despite what you might think, try not to pick a man in the military because you won't think you'll lose him, but you will, before he has a chance to make an honest woman out of you," she instructed, referring to her boyfriend's sudden death before their second daughter and final child together, Mariana, was even born. She was still dealing with the grief of it all two years later as her mom was pushing marriage to a different man with status to provide for her children.

"I won't but will you be okay?" I asked her curiously as she managed to take my long, black dress and cut it to make pant legs, a pantsuit unlike none other in such a short amount of time that worried me but I trusted her.

"I'll be fine if you use all I provided for you in the luggage. There is some cash I put aside for you until you land a job, school details I enrolled you to do summer school that starts today, June 31, something that worked in our favour. I know you did do all your credits here but you'll be safer there with a reputable transcript that works for high school and lots of people," Gloria reassured me with her comforting voice and warm hazel eyes. Unfortunately, similar to my aunts, our goodbye was cut short when police were banging on Gloria's closed bedroom door. She pointed towards a secret side exit she had in the closet and wished me luck as well as told me how she'd always see me as her oldest daughter. This was before she pushed me into the closet and closed the door as soon as she opened the door for the police.

I heard muffled voices as I darted in the dark, unsure of where I was going but was accustomed to being taken away from what I saw as home. I feared the fact that water was covering my feet I only then took notice of were in slippers but kept going until I heard him, the honey-like yet raspy voice of Matthew Chambers I followed in complete trust just because he knew my name when I only began to see light.

I scurried towards his mid-sized wooden boat the moment I saw it, the pant legs undone on what used to be a dress that now had weird cuts in it as I approached a man around my age with a faintly round jawline, shaggy, dirty blonde hair where the straight tips slightly curled along his shoulders. His walnut coloured roots added all the more to the pirate look along with a white, tattered blouse that acted as a dress while he had an eyepatch on, looking as rugged as ever. His shirt was covered in dirt, his hairy legs complimented the outfit along with his muscles that were begging to tear apart the tight blouse that hugged his arms, completely.

"Hey, it's me, the girl you're calling out, Violet!" I projected my voice from afar. "Did a friend of mine send you to bring me to a high school in Marchland?" I asked the handsome man that made it difficult not to think about Chance who I once believed was my everything. I approached the boat closer, gazing into his captivating eyes that put the murky blue water to shame as his ocean blue eyes should've been the sea. I must've been taken away by his dark, sharp eyebrows, thin, dark mustache and what one could barely call a beard with how thin and scattered the dark hairs were, taken away by a pirate saving me because it wasn't me he was looking for.

"I was calling out Scarlet, my second Wednesday girl. We were about to go in for a final round but I double booked today, so I don't mind taking you to a summer school I go to if you let me call her water cab and then we can be on our way," the man who clearly didn't believe in watching TV explained honestly, but did offer me a quick way out of palace grounds which I was grateful for and didn't argue with.

He helped me up onto the boat as I approached the shallow waters it was floating in. I witnessed his shirt float up in the wind to expose tight, blush coloured, lacey, women's panties he was wearing that looked to be a tight fit on his bunched up junk and muscular ass.

"Where's this Wednesday girl?" I mocked him, having a feeling he was pretending to be someone he wasn't with the gentle way he helped me up as he lifted me and placed me on the wooden deck in a delicate manner after taking my luggage from me beforehand.

Our bodies were mere inches from one another but I only thought he was handsome on the outside because my insides were shattered and I didn't even know the guy.

"I don't need that cab, have another fling around the rocky bend," a naked brunette woman with the perfect body came out of a tiny door and dove head first into the brisk water after rubbing herself all over the man in front of me she wished goodbye to. She wouldn't even take his offer of bringing her around the rocky area in the distance.

"Did she only show up in the pair of blush panties you're wearing or why is she swimming away completely naked?" I asked him in complete disgust, having a feeling she was some sort of hooker.

"I like to keep the clothes of those I hook up with as souvenirs, makes me remember all the fun I've had when looking at all the clothes hung in the basement of my boat instead of forgetting so much of it. Everything is labelled too with names on tags I inserted, but you have to admit, she's a fantastic swimmer," he confessed as his eyes were glued to her swimming until she was out of view, weirding me out with his unique fetish.

"Was that a..."

"No, she's not a hooker, just one of the boat girls that parks her own boat around here and hooks up with any guy willing to have her. Not sure who could say no to a body like that though, but that's not the point because you can't go to summer school looking like a tramp with a torn dress exposing your fancy underwear with diamonds on the edges, but I'm sure I have something downstairs for you since my closet of women's clothes is starting to get crowded and pathetic," the obnoxious man with a slight accent that was different than mine, not English but American, Boston to be more precise. Anything he said that ended in a R sounded as if it ended in a H. Despite his interesting accent I was fond of, his kind gestures made him seem less full of himself.

"Why can't I go like this? You're a tramp and seem to be getting a lot of affection and attention," I teased him and he frowned.

"The name's Matthew Chambers or Matt as most people know me. Everyone at the school knows I'm a man whore but won't say it as easily as you had because they want a taste of this," he gestured towards his muscular self. "Don't get me wrong, you'll get much attention, just the wrong kind. Keep putting me in my place and I'll tell you why I sleep with so many woman!" he ordered me.

"What if I don't care or don't want the responsibility of teaching a dick to be less of a dick?" I replied with much sass.

"It's obvious you ran away from somewhere, you don't have to tell me where or even why; it's none of my business. But a suitcase will only get you so far. You can stay here, live with me on my boat for as long or as little as you need. There's only one bedroom though, it's not that big of a boat but there is a hammock by the front, so we can take turns with who gets the bed unless you're fine sharing it. No girls ever sleep over, that's too intimate for me..."

"I'm not a girl, doofus? You only know my name and suddenly think I'll be different than all the girls that want you? You don't know that I'm one to tear blankets out of the bed and roll over constantly because if nobody is there with me, my thoughts keep me awake a lot, especially if I'm further than home from before again!" I defended my dignity.

"Violet, I collect woman's clothes because my ex designs royal clothes at the palace, in particular the queen or any eligible princesses looking for husbands. She could make a new outfit out of something tattered or slutty. She would tell everyone else I was in the military, that I was a duke that got her in, not some high school loser that still has two grade 12 courses left three years after when he was supposed to graduate. She wanted children of her own at a young age, something I wasn't ready for but since I refused to sleep with her for that purpose, she found another way to have children that would look like me. She hooked up with my scum of a brother and got what she wanted, told me to come home when I was ready to be the man she needed. We were in love, just too different and in two different places. Two years ago when my brother got her pregnant again to piss me off, she sent me letters, saying that she had the family she wanted and only needed me and that's when I ended things. Yet I still collect these outfits, hoping I'll find something that she made, a connection to her to see her face one last time because she gave me the courage to build this boat in high school. We were going to venture the world on it until she found a love for fashion, impressed a royal representative of a small palace at one of her shows and suddenly our worlds no longer belonged together," he explained honestly, allowing my heart to sink deep into my chest for him and for the friend I thought I knew.

"It doesn't matter how I know her but she's hung up on you. Her mom is trying to set her up with someone to get her higher up in the palace but she's against it, said you died two years ago and still cries over you. And to prove I know who you're talking about, her name is Gloria O'Neil, Spanish-looking woman with a caring heart. People change with time and sometimes that means you unfortunately grow apart," I gave him the closure he needed and he embraced me in a hug where he practically suffocated me with his muscles and sea water smell but I didn't mind.

"She used to go by Lori when she loved me for me and not the idea of companionship with someone who already knew her well but thanks for telling me that she at least cares to not date so quickly," he let me out of his arms as he breathed in relief that a part of her still cared, that he didn't completely waste his mind, heart and energy on her.

Matt carried on by pulling out a burner phone to call her which I wasn't about to stop him from doing as it was healthier than collecting the clothes of women he slept with.

"Lori, you never speak when I call, only listen, I get it. I'm not a married with kids kind of guy, you knew that about me when you met me. It doesn't matter how I found out, but your mother has your kind of judgement. Let her help you find a suitor that wants what I don't. Let her help you be happy if that's what you need to be happy. We may have grown apart but that doesn't mean you don't matter to me. I have high school to finish and my adventures ahead of me and you have beautiful girls to care for and a man much better than me will swoop you off your feet in no time. Not to mention, more of your designs will be in bigger places one day, I just know it," he encouraged her.

"You think I didn't know that? I was promised that title if I marry the king and we'll venture off to other palace gatherings. I made sure the old queen is far out of his life, planned it as soon as she arrived, even helped the man in the mirror use her to get rid of her, planned the exact day, luggage and everything far in advance, fake documents, all the works. I got over you as soon as you rejected me because it made it clear to me that neither one of us was changing for the other, so it's better we're apart. In a way you helped me become queen and no it hasn't happened yet but I can feel it will. And you won't repeat a word I'm saying because I'll turn you into the cops for your past!" she ripped my heart out of my chest and tore it into tiny pieces she crushed, as if the initial rip didn't inflict enough pain.

"So, you acted sad? You're a fucking bitch and why throw the poor girl into this?" he yelled at her angrily as I stepped further away from him with each step, knowing I needed to find my own way to that school.

"I let her exit the way you used to sneak into the palace to be with me before we were too different. She's probably in the sea, waiting for a boat to come and rescue her, will die there or get caught by the cops and be in jail the rest of her life for killing princess Sophia and the man in the mirror," she began to say and Matt looked at me, not afraid but faintly smiled my direction, knowing who I was and understanding what I was going through. "I wouldn't call anyone on her, just let her live a new life far away. I know from experience that it's better. And I won't repeat what you did but am getting rid of this phone because I'm completely over you now and know that people who commit murders aren't always malicious people and that it was obvious from public broadcasts that that girl needed somewhere to express her true voice and feelings. The castle wasn't it and your revenge for scarring someone like I've been scarred is to realize that as queen and live a miserable life. Bye, Gloria," he ended the call, breathing heavily as he tossed the burner phone into the water and gestured for me to follow him to the basement of the boat which I did. "My alias is Matt, real name was Madison, parents wanted me to be a girl and thought the name still worked since it has the word son in it. I've killed a few people myself and am anything but dangerous but things are easier this way because nobody would understand," he added as we headed down several wooden steps to view a hallway full of metal racks that consisted of all women's clothes.

"You kill any of these women?" I joked as I gestured towards the clothes.

"No," he chuckled. "I killed my dad when he beat my mom more brutal than ever before and then my mom killed herself because she claimed to love him despite how he treated her once they were married. And then my older and only brother, Olie, who was like the parents I never had, took care of me, kept my secret for an hour and then used it against me to get Gloria when she only wanted him for one thing. In a way, I lost him too, just didn't kill him," he shrugged his broad shoulders. "But these clothes are yours because they should be used and this room is also yours; I can take the hammock," he insisted kindly.

I removed the remains of my dress in front of him, not caring I was in my undergarments with how real he got with me and the fact that he was also half naked.

I however didn't go for the clothing on the racks or in my suitcase I had by my side, I removed Matt's eye patch which I tossed on the floor and unbuttoned his white blouse. He fully let go of it, allowing me to take it off him without any questioning or stiffness. The fact that he was wearing nothing but women's underwear, didn't even tempt me because as attractive of a sight it was, I wasn't in a state of mine to desire to savour any of it, in my mind and with my body. I put my arms through the sleeves of the baggy blouse and did up the buttons before asking him to follow me to the room I hardly slept alone in.

"Before we talk more, that looks super tight and uncomfortable. Change and then hold me," I asked him as I opened my suitcase to toss him a pair of my underwear with the diamond trim but a more baggy fit for the material to not get on my nerves, one of the few honest things Gloria did for me.

He let out an airy laugh before putting them on by himself in the hallway and following me into the bedroom with the water bed that caught me off guard but immediately felt like comfort. Matt who soon became Maddy to me in private where nobody else other than us knew his real name, slightly lifted me, making the entire bed vibrate to put his arms around me in a safe way I never desired to be released from.

I craved someone to understand me, every part and although I didn't know much about Matt, I knew he understood something nobody ever would. He understood that murderers aren't always malicious people, that a crime doesn't define you, more so the reason behind it, the reason that person lives over them.

It was made clear Matt was meant to be a protector. As for me, I changed the prophecy because I was made to be a lover, not in the dirty way one assumes, the complete opposite.

I knew just that through the faint yet intimate gazes we exchanged while he was on the phone, not to mention his warm cloth around me that felt like home which verified that.

It was the beginning of my third home, another disappointment because anything I loved so much, I had the habit of losing. Yet again that's why most find it easier to see me as a villain because heroes get happy endings, not just happiness.

The Game

"I understand the guilt even if it felt so right. The man in the mirror was my boyfriend but he only used me to get to Sophia. Yet I deserve that because I should've been faithful to the king, not imagining a life outside of the mirror and wanting to run away with Chance. That was always the plan, him and I going somewhere with no direction, for once not feeling trapped but free, together and free, Maddy," I admitted to him as I sighed in disbelief of all I felt and all I did.

"Maddy?" he asked me puzzled.

"Sorry, I won't say it in front of people or if I do accidentally, I'll say I meant Matty," I slightly paused my rant to let out a breath. "It's just nice to have a secret that won't hurt me for once, that's all," I confided in him.

"I get that and I will never hurt you even if you fall in love with me because I don't do love anymore, don't like negative change, Viola, but that's Violet in public," he opened up to me, only assuming the obvious.

"I'm not the average girl, am not falling for you, just find comfort in you, something that is hard to come by for a girl like me," I voiced to him as he put his finger on my lips when the floor creaked I assumed did that on its own.

"Harmony, please have that be you!" Maddy shouted after gesturing for me to hide under the bed which I did while he grabbed a wooden baseball bat to head towards the danger. However, before he could do any harm with it, the apparent danger approached him.

All I could see from under the bed were Maddy's large bare feet and the smaller feet of a gentleman in sky-blue and white striped high-tops as he dropped his bat.

"Sorry, I didn't think you'd be busy mid-day in women's underwear," a man with a dull voice that was beyond sarcastic was clearly trying to get under Maddy's skin.

"This isn't what it looks like. If you came when I was in a pink pair of underwear that would've been the case," he mocked him in his attempt to defend himself while I couldn't help but burst in laughter and banged my head on the wood holding up the water bed.

"Doesn't sound like your usual skanks, this one snorts," he teased my laugh with his dull voice that his insults made slightly more creative.

I scooted from under the bed, patted down the baggy blouse I was wearing and looked the tall nerd with his round, peach, begging to be punched face with freckles under his eyes and short, flat, stringy, coffee brown hair.

Maddy didn't say one word because without even turning back to look at me. He knew I could handle myself and was a protector in ways that didn't involve his fists.

"Do you have a purpose in being here because I would hardly call us holding and cuddling a skanky move!" I shouted at the man with a mouth full of attitude like my own, heading closer to him with each step to intimidate him as he slowly backed away.

"Okay, okay, I get it. I just wanted to tell Matt that he didn't answer my texts last night and summer school started yesterday, not today. The date was moved last minute and I would have rather worked alone on the group assignment but when I told Mrs. Junes that, she put me with two kids who didn't show up, said I was smart enough to do well and help them. One was you and the other a girl that must be new, Violet Grey," he blabbered.

"What's the project on and when does class start today?" I asked the freckled guy that was irritating me the more he spoke while Maddy and I exchanged a faint smile regarding being in the same group.

"Doesn't matter. I'll do all the work if the new girl says we fooled around," he tempted me but Maddy wouldn't let me shake on it.

"Trust me, you don't want to be known as an easy bang or a quick bang or a whore. I'm not the smartest when it comes to school and books but would redo this year again if it means although you're living here with me, you're seen differently than me," Maddy spoke deep into my soul with words I practically could feel, touch and smell as if they were a physical object.

"He's right. I dealt with my fair share of guy drama so we can do our parts of the project," I stated.

"Alright, class starts in less than an hour and the assignment is due today," he adds.

"Fine I'll let you touch my boob and you'll slap our names onto the assignment," I bargained with him.

"Both and without your bra," he attempted to make things interesting while Maddy gave him a deadly stare.

"You can look at both without the bra, not touch," I tempted him and we shook on it. "Matty, that doesn't give you any permission to do so, so please leave the room," I asked of him.

"Harmony should be here any minute so I'll leave to await her but that doesn't mean I like this or don't want you to speak up or scream if he does anything stupid," Maddy explained as he slightly waved his hand before heading towards the top of the boat.

"You care enough about this law project to show me them?" the pervert with a dashing smile on his face taunted me in a way I could see through.

"What do you really want now that he's out of earshot with who I'm guessing is his girlfriend or the girl he fucks most?" I whispered.

"It's complicated. You remind me a lot of someone I used to know, a girl with a splattered heart tattoo between her uh breasts. I wanted to know if you had the same tat, that's all. I don't need to even see it," he explained and I pulled down the blouse and my bra low enough to not expose my breasts, just the marking between them I exposed by licking my finger to faintly expose it enough to make out what it is.

"Yeah, I have it but whoever you think I am, I'm not. I'm new to this city and got that tat in a private place after a messy breakup," I lied.

"Sure, but you likely have the same one on your lips when the makeup I can tell is there is removed and I'm assuming it's above your vagina too," he blurted out, terrifying me with how much he knew when I barely arrived in an area I believed was a fresh start.

What I did was too fresh to have been put in the news and Gloria was the only one who knew about the markings and couldn't have revealed that so quickly, or did she?

I stood there so frozen, so numb that my body could've easily been taken away and pronounced dead. However, that was when it hit me that Sophia wasn't dead, so stunned that she appeared lifeless but wasn't, that's why she wasn't smiling. She witnessed it all and desired to have me dead, if not put behind bars. That man was planning to do both as I noticed a recording device tucked into his checkered shirt that had a few wires sticking out. There was also the fact that no man's private area popped out that much. It was likely he had a gun in his pants.

"I've been trapped my entire life. If you're going to do one of the two, shoot me, or better yet, hand me the gun so I can do it myself," I managed to voice to him strongly, meaning every word I said. That was when he stuck his hand down his loose, camel coloured jeans and pulled out a revolver and held it up to his temple and shot himself, an option I didn't even think of. "Why?"

"Now you'll know you really did kill two people and that guilt will make you feel more trapped than prison," the voice that was anything but dull, beyond cryptic, spoke and Maddy darted down the stairs as soon as he heard the gunshot and it was then that a goon of Sophia's was dead.

I tried to feel for a pulse but nothing was there, his chest wasn't moving and his hands and skin quickly felt like ice. I sobbed over the man for another crime I didn't intend to commit but Maddy pulled me away and threw me into his arms.

"Hey, stop it! He killed himself; that had nothing to do with you, so don't worry your pretty face about it," he held me closely in his arms as a woman with wavy, caramel hair that hugged her shoulders approached us closer. Part of her hair was done back and a blueish purple coloured barrette pushed her hair back. The barrette matched the tank top with the frilly trim she was wearing. She had on a light grey hoodie that was missing its sleeves, exposing her pale shoulders, and she wore mid-length jean shorts, pulling the chill look together along with her bulky headphones that landed above the cleavage her tank top displayed. The way her greenish blue eyes gazed at Maddy when he held me said she loved him and wasn't going to snitch on what happened even if he didn't want a real relationship with her.

"Harmony, Matt's morning make out sess and you either really hate Anderson or he tried something while you were waiting for Matt to come back and finish what he started since I'm assuming that's why he's in your underwear," she held her hand out that wasn't on his shoulder to shake mine.

"Didn't even know his name. He was being very creepy and when I called him out for having a gun in his pants, he shot himself," I admitted most of the truth to her while Maddy read between the lines, holding me all the tighter. "And we barely cuddled; I'm no threat, just staying here with Matty after running away from home for very good reasons although parts of home apparently haven't left," I sighed and the girl whose voice sounded as inviting and angelic as her name, joined our embrace.

"We'll never be serious but thanks, hun, and this is your new home no matter what certain people say," she faintly smiled, welcoming me and I smiled back.

"We can either dump his body here, away from the school or leave him here and deal with him later," Maddy suggested and the three of us knew what we had to do as we wrapped him in a spare blanket with the gun, mopped up the few drops of blood that weren't on him but the wooden floors and tossed him overboard. We were careful to tie him in the blanket with thick rope that was used for fishing purposes before throwing his heavy body into the depths of the water together.

It was then that Harmony offered to steer the boat towards the school, giving Maddy and I a chance to change downstairs.

"Are you okay after everything?" he reassured me in front of the rack of clothes.

"Stunned but okay, and you? Oh, and Harmony seems nice, why are you letting Gloria control your love life?" I barely gave him a chance to answer the first question as I eagerly waited to hear the answers to both.

"I've seen worse, done worse, am okay too. But me and Harmony has nothing to do with Gloria. There were bits and pieces of that I finally got answers to today but I don't believe a world as fucked up as this, where you have to hide from your criminal activity as if it defined you when your emotions for yourself or someone else were in control, not you, deserves more people in it. I don't want anyone to have to undergo what I did, what you did, and we became a friends with benefits thing a while ago, when things with Gloria became rocky, three years ago. I knocked Harmony up, Viola, and I told her that I couldn't live with myself if we kept the baby but she did anyway, said I'd see the beauty in life I could never completely find. I respected her decision since it's her body but the baby helped us in actually being in a real relationship and she ended up miscarrying at 12 weeks. We didn't even plan to tell her parents until we were sure and never told them anything since her three month ultrasound ended. That tore us apart. I never told her why I don't want kids, just that it wasn't part of the plan although her pregnancy changed things then and we can never be just friends after that because we both feel like we had a child we lost. We talk and kiss and stuff every morning to feel that closeness, but I'll never have sex with her again after what happened. And it's hard to get close again to someone who wished you didn't exist because you were the one to cause pain since a bad condom wasn't enough," he opened up to me as he removed my underwear to put on his own, along with jean shorts and an open, pale blue button-up top to show off his gorgeous abs and slightly hairy chest.

"She was going through stuff, as were you. She didn't mean a word of it, I can tell you that much," I reassured him, my eyes not leaving his for a second as I followed his lead and put on an off the shoulder white dress with a snowy hill-like trim along the neckline, sleeves and bottom, where it ended above my knees. The pure dress instantly turned dark, turned black and I felt it, felt the idea of my soul being degraded but ignored it.

"You didn't look at my junk like most girls, instead my eyes, only my eyes, so I don't tell anyone what I'm going to tell you, but will anyway because I know you won't repeat it. I don't even have to ask you to swear on it or blackmail you but Harmony changed because of me, that's why I can barely take a breath when talking about her, need to say it all in one shot, rip it off like a bandage that has been there for far too long..."

"Like a magical change, like my dress?" I interrupted him, knowing the secret of my own was also a huge factor in him being able to talk to me so easily.

"I tried to drown myself when we met, didn't see a point in living anymore after feeling so lost when I wanted to be someone I wasn't for Gloria but knew I couldn't. I was drunk when I did this and a woman with the most beautiful singing dove in and saved me. I couldn't make out her figure since my vision was blurred but it was her because I recognized her gentle touch when her voice vanished for a while. We communicated with notes, our eyes and bodies and practically had our own language until conceiving a child restored her voice. She saved my life, gave me a new appreciation for it and in return I gave her back her voice but not our creation, stuff that wouldn't have happened if I really checked the condom before putting it on," he sighed while covering his hand over his face, as if ashamed of his past. I forced his hand to return to his side and stared into the depths of his ocean blue eyes. "What?" He barked at me.

"The what is your past doesn't matter when you have the present in your hands that controls the future. If you really want her in your life, you'll find a way that might hurt, but might also heal," I attempted to comfort him as he held my arms and ran his fingers along the ruffled edges on my sleeves.

"Crows aren't terrible or bearers of bad news but they show that everlasting love is possible. I do read once in a while, don't judge, do today, not tell," he muttered words I didn't quite understand but realized how important they were when we slipped on a pair of shoes and shortly after it stopped, exited the boat.

"So I take it as we'll be failing the Law project?" I asked Maddy an obvious question I knew the answer to.

"Yeah, but I'm used to it," he sighed. "It seems to mean a lot to you since you were willing to let Andy see your tits," he correctly assumed.

"I want the world to be less of an injustice and I want to be a part in making that happen. That was my goal as queen but even with that power, I couldn't do much. But maybe as a lawyer or someone with the job to defend others, I can and it all starts with being able to take an actual Law course that universities can look at," I confessed to a man I sensed had dreams one also wouldn't expect.

"Lawyer, murderer or not, I can't not see you as a queen because you're tough and went through a lot to obtain the best image you could yet still have enough confidence to speak your mind," he voiced in a kind and genuine manner to me as we headed upstairs after I fetched my school schedule Gloria set up for me. We then went to exit the boat Harmony parked in front of the large, beige coloured school with a dirt walking path surrounding it. "So, I'll see you at lunch as usual and maybe between classes I can trace my tongue along your tits and…"

"I don't want to hear the end of that or your voice to sound so seductive and turned on by your own words! On lunch, he's having a mini date with you since it'll be short but the start of something new that puts the past aside and rekindles the look you give him he looks away during every time even when he starts the conversation because he doesn't want to feel your soul and desire all parts of you with the idea of commitment present. He knows with how much you two have been through that it can't be casual and that he's afraid of what will happen if he doesn't get hurt for a change," I looked out for his best interest while he gazed into her eyes that lit up by the sight of his own.

"One lunch because Violet is a pain in my ass, that's the only reason," Maddy emphasized, throwing a half smile her direction as suddenly her mouth ended up in his and he embraced it, not holding back as he smothered it with much hunger as his desperate and selfish eyes took over despite how risky it was for them to be so fast with things again that needed more time and nourishment.

He began to run his fingers through the waves of her hair that resembled the current of the sea that ended where the school began. His hand that wasn't in her hair, stroked her chin as she began to undo the buttons of his shirt. He dropped his hand from her hair to rip the thin material of her blueish purple tank top in half to reveal her cheddar orange bra with a sky-blue bow. Maddy proceeded by using a pocket knife he always made sure to have on him when clothed, to ruin her bra, cut it in half and bury his head in her breasts as he removed all fabric on her top half in the matter of seconds.

"I'd recommend not showing your bare asses to the entire school who have a good view of where you're standing on the boat but you do you. See you later. I have classes to attend to and new people to meet," I stated my honest opinion and added the last part in utter excitement for what my potential new home held.

"Be there in time to do my internship as the Art teacher's assistant. For now, we have an entire half hour to express our own emotions in a way paper or paint can't feel for us," Harmony broke apart from Maddy for a few seconds to mutter between giggles when he said how he didn't care if the entire school saw his ass because he was finally back with her, completely.

I made my way off the boat, knowing they were treating that half hour as if it were their last, as I turned around to see two completely bare bodies going at it as Maddy leaned on the steering wheel. The boat moved as they did until it slightly tilted and they continued what they started in the water while I took steps forward, not backwards or so I assumed.

"I finished the project and maybe my partners will contribute next time, the girl at least since Matt will likely fail another year of summer school if every intern or teacher makes reality not exist for him," I overheard a dull, familiar voice tease Maddy's abilities to a middle-aged teacher with her chestnut brown hair tied in a loose bun and her pale blue dress shirt and charcoal black, mid-length skirt add to her professional look.

"Thomas Anderson, that's the least of your worries. You woke up almost drowning, tied up in a blanket and survived except you only remember bits and pieces from yesterday and nothing from the days before with your diagnosis of dissociative amnesia. I recommend you take some time off from summer school to rest, relax and rejuvenate, the three Rs," the woman with the upbeat voice chuckled at her own joke I didn't believe was even funny enough to be called a joke.

It was then he dismissed her, rolled his eyes and the voice that seemed so familiar yet I couldn't place it, bumped into me, not his voice, his body, his wet, bruised body.

"Is this your first time taking summer school because I've never seen you here before?" the man revealing himself to be Anderson with a bandage on his bullet wound and several bruises on his face and spaghetti-like arms, asked me.

Although I wasn't exactly certain as to how much he remembered, I couldn't help but place my fingers on the bruises on his face out of guilt while his soothing sterling grey eyes made me feel numb in a way guilt had no play in. His short and stringy, coffee brown hair had more of a wave to it with the way the sea parted it so more of the moist wave was on the right side than the left. Unlike Maddy's rugged beard, he had a faint shadow that didn't look as if he shaved it but as if he couldn't grow facial hair. Anderson's face was much more round, not chiselled or easy to punch as I first assumed. I first took notice that he had as much rage as I did about life with one look into his solemn eyes.

"How much of today do you remember, Andy?" I asked him in concern as I kissed his bruises.

"Nothing. Even yesterday, I only know about the assignment because a pen with soggy notes but somewhat legible notes from it was in my jean pocket. I hardly remember the last week but everything before that, I know for the most part. I thought I was having a nightmare, woke up to be trapped in a blanket with rope in the water, don't know how I didn't drown, but that I must've woken up very quick. The fucker who tied me up didn't check my pockets. I had a small fishing spear on me since after school, it's a fun hobby of mine in the sea. I used it to cut a big enough slit to loosen the rope even more and swam to a nearby cove where I rang a bell for help and was brought to school. There was a gun with me but the fuckers filled it with fake blood not bullets, so someone didn't want me dead," I felt more confused the more he spoke at what his original intentions were, why he desired to fake a death but tossed that thought to the side for a later date because I was far from done with him.

"I'm sorry, babe, to hear that and I'll help you search for the fucker that did this to you because you might be alive but forget all about me, about us! Why would they do this?" I whined like a little girl, hoping he'd buy what I was attempting to sell.

"You're stunning and you're my girlfriend? I'm sorry but I might not remember things but have trouble believing I wouldn't remember that," his insecurities truly showed.

"We didn't label things but I got the wrong date of when summer school started, didn't show up yesterday and ran into you this morning after you found Matthew Chambers's boat to yell at him for getting the day wrong since you were assigned to be partners with him in your Law class and did all the work. We met there because he offered me a place to stay on his boat since I ran away from home for good reasons. I introduced myself, Violet Grey, and you mentioned we'd also be working together but you'd help us out with this assignment and we'd contribute for the rest. We spoke for a while about old crime cases, our opinions on that and really clicked. I asked you out to do something after school and you said yes, called me babe as a joke since we already seemed to know each other so well, so I called you babe back, thought it might trigger something and wish you didn't head back to the school by yourself because then maybe we'd both lose our memory and feel as close as earlier because we'd have something huge in common," I blabbered a somewhat believable lie to him without even grinding my teeth or letting a smile slip, that's how good I got at the craft of retelling the truth. I was ashamed of this but if it makes one feel better, I got the ending I deserved.

"I don't know what I told you but I'm a little rusty in certain areas but am willing to read any books or manuals you have in mind," he proved himself to be more of a nerd the more he spoke.

I lightly snickered as a response. "We just met and I don't do that stuff right away with a guy and I just want you to be yourself. And worst-case scenario if you are bad in bed, we'll be bad in bed together," I teased and he held my hand in his.

"You're sweet but I kind of have a rule when getting involved with a woman," he admitted, intriguing me.

"And what's that?" I asked him curiously, nervously twisting strands of my hair.

"She has to play my all-time favourite game with my friends and I at lunch and if she can survive it, we can go out on our first date tonight of possibly many. I guess I forgot to mention that this morning," he explained honestly.

"Yeah, you must've," I lied. "Uh, what's this game?" I asked him curiously, nerves slightly creeping up on me as I sensed it wouldn't be simple.

"It's truth or dare but we don't exactly play it fair. It's not a clean version or conflict free," he admitted.

"There's hardly anything I'd say no to doing or even saying. I'll be fine," I shrugged my shoulders.

"Cool. Until then, we can see each other at lunch, the first table to the left when you walk in the cafeteria, that's where we'll play, and see you in Law second period, after lunch," he said with a quick wave before heading towards the school across from the sea, the large school that I wished the people of Edgebrook could get to because then maybe they'd have a chance.

I waved back but doubted he saw it as I was on a hurry to get towards the boat to ask Maddy to hand me my schedule I left in my suitcase on the boat as I noticed he finished things up with Harmony as the two of them were in each other's underwear on the hammock, Harmony's bare chest pressed against Maddy's as they took in the relaxation and their beating hearts.

That didn't seem to get their attention but the next part allowed Maddy to bring the boat closer to me so I didn't have to swim with how far they let it drift out. "Overboard isn't overboard," was all I had to shout out for them to know exactly what I was referring to.

I quickly boarded the boat as soon as it approached me and I explained my plan since his memory appeared to be partly erased. Maddy immediately warned me. "Your plan is good because one's enemies must be kept closer so you'll have something on him if he remembers everything but I've seen that group game played by them before. It can get really bad, but you'll be okay if you follow two rules. Don't choose any truths or say no to anything," he looked out for me.

"Why those two rules? I never played his fucked up games," Harmony added, thinking the same as I did.

"Well, I had three years back before I created a name for myself my own way. Truths get really personal, questions you've never been asked in your life but know the answer to and those are secretly recorded, used as blackmail. As for saying no to things, like a dare, you'll be given a truth that's worse and if you don't want to do either, you will be shoved head first into the massive compost bins in the cafe that reek. You won't be able to get the smell out for weeks, get out of the bin on your own and won't be trusted to play the game again, be in his life. I wouldn't even get involved in this but the fact that the gun didn't have bullets like you mentioned says this guy wants you to play games. I advise you to play them in a way that plays him," Maddy projected his voice to me as he passed Harmony her clothes and bra which she quickly put on while he covered her. Once dressed, Maddy went to grab my suitcase and came back with my schedule, nothing else he questioned me about because it wasn't his business.

"You have Law second but what do you have first?" I asked him curiously.

"Sex education," he said in confidence while throwing his clothes on from before that had two buttons undone to show off his abs with hardly any hair covering them.

Harmony hit him in the arm after she zipped up her faded jean shorts. "Ignore his sarcasm, he's taking gym. His dream is to be an athlete the world recognizes, like in the Olympics or something," she corrected his humour I didn't need to be corrected because I understood it since I was known to be snarky, anything but walked all over.

"Enjoy learning about sex in that case and then Harmony can be your practice when you get back," I teased him in slight laughter he joined in on.

"Alright but it won't be as much fun as learning about orgasms in your class," he joked again after glancing at my schedule and Harmony rolled her eyes at his play on words.

"He isn't wrong. Biology is all about the study of life and to create more life, species must pro-create and maybe a toad or two can let out a few orgasms while they're at it," I teased, allowing Maddy to snicker before Harmony pulled his arm.

"You're passing this year and will be the first in your family to do something meaningful with your life," she assured him as they headed towards the school, her arms clenched onto his. Maddy turned around to stick his tongue out, proving that sometimes life is taken too seriously that you forget to make memories that make it worth living. He also gave me a thumbs up I assumed was a sign of good luck for the game I didn't realize was already in play.

I exited the boat with my schedule and a few notepads Maddy passed me from my suitcase to take class notes when a guy with ginger coloured hair running with metal scissors sniped one of the longer front pieces of my short hair before running off.

"Why?" I asked him, surprised by the strange behaviour as I chased after him but another guy got in my way when he asked if I could kiss him.

"First, he cuts my hair then you want to kiss me? What in God's name is going on here?" I asked the sandy haired boy with a slim figure and short height.

"You're the only girl in today's game and the game has started for us but your dares and truths will begin at lunch. You're new and any co-ed dares involve you. The dares are random, from a bucket, so you don't know who put them in there. Mine was to kiss the girl playing and if I don't do this, I have to tell the group my biggest secret and I can't do that," he nervously rambled.

"Then make one up. If you believe your own lie, so will everyone else, just don't make it too real since it can be used against you. But if you're not finding this game fun, why are you in this group? Why are you playing if you don't have something at stake, a relationship like myself?" I asked him in wonder.

"When you're in this group, you don't go home every day with rashes in your ass crack because you constantly get wedgies! You don't get black eyes because you're beat up, and you don't get bad mouthed so much that you have no friends. This group controls the school and once you're in, you can choose to sit out of these games unless money or something else is a prize," he admitted to me honestly.

"Okay, I'll kiss you," I said, feeling for the boy, but had my own agenda as well. "But you need to answer something for me first," I stated and he nodded desperately.

"Anything at all, Ms.," he replied in a fast pace.

"You can call me Violet," I said kindly as he held out his hand to shake, shocking mine in the process, so much so that I couldn't let go.

My hand went as numb as my body did as I passed out shortly after on the concrete. It was as if my body went into some state of shock to process the waves of electricity and when I regained my consciousness shortly after to feel as if I was in a body of water but in actuality was on Maddy's water bed. I opened my eyes slowly due to the immense aches my body felt that was bandaged up where it felt most sensitive, where bruises laid. I sat up to notice I wasn't in my black dress but a light jean, mid-length one from Maddy's closet of hookups, with ruffly sleeves and a low-cut neckline, even my undergarments were different as they weren't black but a dark grey. I grabbed my notebooks that were next to me and gazed at a bright yellow sticky note on one.

Too dangerous. No game. Right table at lunch instead to talk.

- T.A

Under the sticky note was a photograph of my unconscious body on the concrete which had the fabric cut straight down, likely by the guy with the scissors. My only question was why me?

My only answer was because you killed and when one kills, it doesn't go away, it follows. But Thomas Anderson saving a girl like me, a girl who kills, doesn't save or stop like him.

What happens when his memory is returned? Will he still see me as this damsel, hard worker and determined woman that gets what she believes is entitled to her or the monster I don't even recognize when that guy sniped a lock of my hair because it looked too dark to be me?

He did have a fake gun, maybe he wasn't hired to hurt me or chose to do the exact opposite. Yet one will never know where one's intentions may lie because two minds never fully cross.

The Freeing Blueprint

I left the note and picture behind on Maddy's bed in case something happened to me and made my way towards the large sand coloured building I made my way inside this time.

The inside of the building was as spacious as the outside, a four-floor building, one floor just being designed for science equipment, the only floor I explored until lunch.

There was so much room on that floor alone or it could've been the lack of students as each student received their own lab station and teacher. It may have been a lonely class but was so hands on, one could easily forget that.

Gloria may have lost my trust in what she did but she knew me so well that it honestly didn't scar me. She knew I wasn't meant to be trapped in a castle and knew Biology would help me in a field of fighting for what is right due to that science providing much of the evidence.

It was good to start off with a course I only had to compete against myself in because Law was competitive and lunch was overwhelming.

I vividly remember leaving the Science floor with goggle marks around my eyes as I made my way upstairs to the main floor with the cafeteria.

I marched up the cement grey coloured stairs that reminded me too much of the situation I hardly remembered outside until a guy with a larger figure and height that towered me said something so utterly painful.

"You're the girl who almost was raped. I'm sorry but next time wear a dress that shows less of your titties or don't wear a dress at all if you're asking for it," he stopped my heart for several seconds at that obscene word I hoped I'd never have to hear my name in front of again.

I took a deep breath in and out before confronting him since I disagreed with his point and wasn't going to back down. "I don't remember what happened, wasn't conscious when it almost happened but know I could have worn a snowsuit and received the same results. The dress I'm wearing now might be a little revealing too but it's just fat, just skin, my skin I shouldn't be afraid to show because assholes like you can't keep their mouse in its house!" I stood up for myself while mocking him at the same time and when he was about to throw himself at me, I beat him to it.

I twisted his wrists behind his back and asked him if his mother would be proud of how he's treating women. Before he could answer and I loosened my grip on him, did his hands escape and attempt to reach for my breasts until a tranquilizing gun hit him on the head and he fell into a deep slumber.

"You can't always keep your enemies close, Viola," a taunting voice tickled my ear, that was playing me the entire time.

"I don't know what you're talking about," I denied the words of the silver eyed freak who faked his memory loss and exposed it so suddenly.

"Okay, so you're telling me that this doesn't change things," he asked as he handed me his phone which displayed my half naked body that had the splattered heart marks I forgot about because he made them disappear with a photo editing tool. "I told the king I thought I found the girl but was wrong," Anderson surprised me more his actions. "And before you ask, I have my own problems too and have a conscience, that's why I didn't send the real picture I gave you," he added.

"Bet that's why you faked your death too but why tell me this at all?" I asked him perplexed.

"I have debt I owe but realized putting someone in a jail cell is like taking away their life away and I know you deserve a life and that I'll get my money in a different way," he confessed to me, leaving me concerned about what kind of mess he landed himself in.

"How much debt is it? Where are you living right now?" I asked him in concern as he attempted to walk away and head up the stairs that were next to where we were standing.

"Doesn't matter. You're not my girlfriend and therefore it's not your problem," he brushed me off but

I felt as if it was my place to look after him and followed him up the stairs until he turned around at the halfway point of the secluded stairway most students didn't use. "If it means you will leave me alone, my old girlfriend scammed me and that's all I'm going to leave it as. I help clean after school and in exchange have a classroom all to myself until school the next day, my mini apartment. It beats sleeping on friends's couches, ran away from a bad home situation when I was 12," he mumbled, shrugging his shoulders to make it appear like it was nothing, ashamed to admit the vague yet tough words I felt the wound they left as I had similar wounds.

"You could've had money to give yourself a really good life. Why give me a chance when as I'm sure the king who I knew wasn't completely on my side but didn't think would take measures regarding everything so quickly, told you everything about me and Chance, the guy who used me to exit the mirror and get to Sophia, the girl he actually loved, who I have a feeling is still alive. And I ran away to start fresh, feel free, have control of where it is I want to go. I don't really have much of a life to save with the burden of killing someone on my mind and desiring to live in those moments that were real to me but fake to him forever. I honestly won't hate you if you go for the money because maybe being more trapped and disciplined than before is what I need," I voiced my insecurities to a man I didn't expect to understand me.

I still remember the look on his face when I said that. It was a doubtful look but not regarding my words because he didn't look at me or the ground but into space, his mind, reflecting on his actions. "The game wasn't supposed to get so out of hand, was only supposed to get information from you I could use in a court to put you behind bars. If that dingbat didn't drug you with the stuff he put on your hands when he shook it with an electric jolt thingy to make it seem like something it wasn't, we wouldn't be talking so civil right now. He wanted to rape you, not find subtle ways to look at your markings. I pulled you away and let the bullies of the school beat the culprit to shreds since I can't fight for shit. Even then, I was going to bring you back to where you're currently living, clean up your bruises from when you weren't completely unconscious and tried to fight him, let you rest and call the cops so you'd be in custody when you wake up. But I opened your suitcase by the bed to dress you because you didn't deserve to see the tattered clothes on your body, the exposed bruises, no human did. I grabbed a dress I'm assuming was custom made and grabbed you underwear and a bra I found in there and saw a picture of your parents with notes on the back from your aunts. I felt like an orphan too and you had your parents taken away from you, your aunts and then a guy that tore you apart even more. You need a chance to find what it means to be you despite all you have done and all that has been done to you because that can't be taken away from you," he confessed much that made me feel uncomfortable although the sentiment that someone cared meant something.

"You saw me naked and went through my stuff so much so that you read personal letters my aunts put on the back of photos! I know you don't realize this but in a place where I shouldn't feel trapped, you managed to do just that without a jail cell! You already got me to show so much of myself to you with hardly knowing me and the last person that I opened up to so much overtime made me a monster in everyone's eyes but my own and well, Matty, that's what makes living so difficult," I teared up and he looked at my eyes in an alarmed manner. "I know, I cry blood now. If you expect to be in my life after all you did, touching my bare skin without my consent and reading stuff that doesn't belong to you, you won't run from me and I'll even see if Maddy is fine with you living with us on the boat because it's better than having to pretend you showed up to class early and aren't living there," I let my bloodshot tears seep into my skin, the red completely vanishing as Anderson whispered the name of the man who attempted to force himself upon me and told me several times that he managed to get him charged with some jail time and that he'd be willing to do the same if it meant I felt comfortable to be around him. That was when I stood on the same step as him and grabbed his hand to spread his fingers apart and place my fingers in his own. "I think we could try to get along, maybe even be friends but girlfriend and boyfriend at school. I am good at physical fights when I don't let my guard down, let my words sting others when they need to and you have connections at this school, have the ability to cancel games or get bullies involved and for survival purposes, I think we could help each other," I suggested and that was when he moved his lips towards mine, allowing my stomach to fall in fear and grief. But before I could even control the spirals of emotions that made me slightly nauseous, did he brush off some dust of the sleeve of my dress.

"Didn't realize how dusty this stairwell was but your proposal might just work for me except Matt and I aren't on the greatest terms since Harmony is my sister and I know she can do so much better than a guy who got her pregnant and didn't even offer to marry her or try to give her more than a boat. Then he just displays physical affection with her when he feels like it; that's hardly a relationship if you ask me and I can't see her that heartbroken again, especially with him wearing your underwear and you wearing his white pirate-like shirt. He's not committed to Harmony if he can get that close to a woman and treat it as if he did nothing, like his entire relationship with my sister. I wouldn't mind keeping an eye on him and talking to you more but I wouldn't bet my life on him agreeing to it," Anderson admitted something that made things much more complicated and made me wonder if something that didn't feel sexual to me but familiar was the same for Maddy or if I was another girl to give him attention.

"How much do boats cost around here? What if we got our own?" I suggested the moment that unsettling thought appeared in my head.

"There's an old boat yard where I'm sure if we spend enough time there, we can make a boat beautiful for close to nothing but it'll take time and we'd need somewhere to live until then. It can be our secret side project until then because I know Matt and know when a girl is just being used for a future hookup," he confessed to me and that lunch we ate some of the cafeteria pizza that was free for summer school students and I told him my vision for our boat. This was all while he sketched it out, being a much better drawer than me, except he didn't draw a boat but a house.

I gazed at the paper in awe at how much promise it had and then around the cream coloured cafeteria walls, then the smokey grey table, across the room to find my eyes wander in the blue seas of Maddy's orbs. I faintly smiled his way as I witnessed him laughing with a bunch of other jocks and girls in skimpy outfits but no Harmony in sight.

"If she laughs any harder I think her boobs will fall out of her non-existent bra and I think you might be right about him since he did even tease me once to not fall in love with him," I joked and sighed at my realization as my eyes focused on Anderson's sterling grey eyes full of dark clouds circling them but stars hidden behind them allowed them to sparkle.

"Yep, that's Matt for you. He won't fall in love but will let girls fall for him, wants them to fall for him to feel some satisfaction in his life but won't let himself become that vulnerable, leaving them confused and heartbroken. Harmony and I are siblings that lived different lives since she stayed at home and I took off and we stayed in contact when I started at the same summer school as her but I care about her as much as any brother. Matt even has a rule to not let women sleep over after intimate activity because that's too close for him. I'd really like to know what kind of lousy parents he had!" he rolled his eyes as a group of guys asked him about the game and he told them that he could make friends without that and desired no part in it.

"Thanks for that, and his parents were more than lousy but that isn't my story to tell. I could easily be the same way but am trying to be as open to new possibility as I can be because I'm not in that palace anymore," I explained and he nodded.

"It wasn't just about you but about me following my dreams with no distractions and this can be our palace. It's not a boat because I don't want to move anymore, stay in one comfortable spot and I know you want the same. There's a scrap yard, I don't see why we can't build our own house. I'm trying to get into construction anyways and that's the best way to start since I'll have to wait a while to get a college education and am working there anyways but don't need school if I can work my way up. I'm just living at the school because I didn't have enough for rent to keep my apartment and kind of don't want to go back once I save up a bit more again, it didn't feel like my own. I can even get you a job there if you want the money for school if you're not afraid to get a little dirt on your fingers. I'm just sick of being realistic, so building my own home would be a dream and having someone special to keep me on my toes and share it with me just makes it better," he couldn't help but grin without his teeth looking as if he felt the completion his life lacked.

"I'm in; if I was afraid of a little dirt, I'd be dead, have dealt with much worse," I sighed and Anderson lightly grazed the back of my neck, under my hair with his fingertips. "Can we go after school to ask if they're looking for anyone new to join the team? Any money will help me with the tuition for January's term once I apply and finish summer school with a good Science course and an actual Law course under my belt that will make me ideal in the eyes of any university," I asked and admitted one of my personal goals to him as it was only fair.

"Sure, if you can ask Matt if I can live with you both temporarily," he bartered with me as we had a habit of doing.

"That won't be a problem but there's only one bed and a hammock," I didn't mind him bartering but had to tell him there'd be a slight chance that Maddy and I would be in the same bed.

"I've seen what goes on in that hammock. Three of us can be in a bed, not a huge deal if you don't make fun of my onesie..."

"There's a spare bed that is very old that isn't used. You two can sleep in that since my hammock is apparently too good for Anderson and he doesn't trust me with a girl in the same bed as me. Then you can build whatever the fuck this is and leave my life because it's obvious I'm destined to not understand and feel true, genuine human connection," Maddy stated in envy behind us as he stared at the page in my notebook that looked like a blueprint of the inside of a house. Inside it were three bedrooms, one for us, and two for our children as we both had the same vision that we'd be with someone and it would end in a heartbreak and we'd help each other raise the children we were left with. It was only the bedrooms he began to sketch out, no fun rooms yet or many items in them and Maddy already thought I replaced him.

"Wait! This won't be for a long time and is pure imagination! I'm not replacing you and feel that kind of connection with you! We have stuff in common that isn't easy to find and it's hard for a girl like me to find warmth and comfort like that when her home life was so broken and she doesn't even know where home is!" I shouted my words all the louder as he walked away, shaking his wavy locks back as if he was better than me while some students laughed, others booed and most said he had emotions and was boyfriend material.

I craved to chase after him and talk to him but Anderson stopped me by putting his hand that was on my neck on my own hand when I attempted to leave the table. "You're beginning to let people see through his shield. He wants you to only see him, not everyone to see him and wants you to not let other's see you. But it doesn't matter what he wants; it's what you want that matters," Anderson voiced to me kindly, giving me the control I always believed my life lacked while brushing his hand against mine, allowing soothing vibration to enter my body.

"I want a playroom for the kids so they always have an excuse to be together and never feel alone. I want a lawyer's office, kitchen with every appliance imaginable since when I lived in Edgebrook, we barely had any food and in the palace, everything was so fancy and made for me. I'd want to try every kind of cooking and baking device for myself, have say in what enters my body. I want a cosy sofa for family time and movie nights, a bookshelf to not read books but to write stories to tell the kids that can help them when we felt most alone. I want a walk-in shower with a view of nature to really detox from the world and the closet for the bedroom can be not massive but not tiny either, average, just like the house that will be average but have so much personality that will change that," I explained, thinking about only myself for a change.

"Alright, I like all that, let's just add a backyard with a mini baseball diamond, had one growing up. It was my favourite thing about my childhood home besides my sister. Oh and we must have bamboo pillows because I heard those are the most comfortable thing and feel the need to be the judge of that," Anderson got as into the house as I did and our smiles met before the bell rang to indicate it was the end of lunch. It was then that Anderson promised to finish the drawing and tucked it into his notebook which was under mine as he insisted to carry mine to class to convince everyone that we were indeed a couple.

However, it wasn't those around us that needed convincing but ourselves with the project we were assigned as soon as we walked up a staircase and entered the first door on the left that truly tested us.

We took seats next to each other and Maddy was already sitting in front of us, gazing back at us until the teacher entered the room.

"If you have something to say, just say it!" I yelled at him in complete irritation.

"Fine!" he huffed. "Out of everyone here to fuck, you had to choose someone who hates me so much and will make it so hard for us to stay friends!" he wrongfully assumed.

"We're only friends but there's no telling what we'll do in the future," I teased and as soon as Maddy caught a glimpse of Anderson's smirk, did he jump on his own desk and then was about to leap towards us to give Anderson a piece of his mind until the teacher spoke up as she entered the room.

"I think we found our group that will be doing the hardest beginner assignment at home," she taunted us in her beyond heavy English accent as she handed Maddy an actual baby the moment he received the hint from her to use self-control.

"Whose child is this and what does this have to do with Law?" he questioned the teacher that looked as if she could've been in high school herself while he struggled calming the cranky baby who looked to be around six or seven months.

"You three are excused from class and can read the instructions that excuse you from this class for a week," she dismissed us in her squeaky voice.

Before I could even have a chance to understand what was going on, I was handed a seven page document titled, "Parenting Is Like A Case". It was then that I knew that we were assigned a real life baby project except two of us did more than just the case.

I didn't expect to get over Chance so quickly but when something only makes you feel safe, not necessarily completely happy or in love, your attachment can easily be lost in a week or in my case less.

What occurred was unexpected for me but not for the guy who watched the entire thing unfold. He noticed the chemistry, had the right to be afraid to lose me because in a room of only the three of us, I wouldn't gravitate towards him as much as I used to. But who could blame me when one said everything I ever felt the need to hear, so much so that I thought I couldn't ask for anything better. Yet again, I did mention I got what I deserved.

The Baby Project

"Rock the fucking screaming thing! I tried everything and Violet said she'd change his diaper if we could calm the baby down. I don't want to change her diaper, not sure about you!" Maddy yelled at Anderson the moment we were dismissed from class with the instructions for the project and a package full of enough diapers, formula as well as milk, and clothes to last the week.

"I know her name's Viola. I tried so many schemes with her but couldn't do it. But calming a baby, that I can do," he shocked Maddy when we reached outside as he stole the baby girl out of his arms and ran towards the sea, leaving Maddy and I to discuss what I didn't have a chance to tell him.

"How connected to your past is this guy? Damage to my image aside, can he be trusted?" I was asked what one would assume was a difficult question in my position yet I didn't even hesitate with my answer.

"He was hired after the king apparently tried to help me escape, seems a little out of character for him but the guy betrayed me with how much authority I had to change the lives of our people, so I wouldn't put it past him to backstab me or for his daughter who I have a feeling is alive to convince him to go after me. But he knows what I look like after what I did, so it doesn't make sense but I don't know why else he'd be hunting me. A part of me wants to say he is using me for something I can't place yet but everyone has and I have a really good feeling that he wouldn't have drawn that sketch if he didn't want to be in my life. So, I trust him and we have a project to do, an insane project that you have to put your differences aside for, but you'll get through," I admitted honestly and reassured him.

Maddy scoffed. "You're horny and only want his naked body next to yours in either my bed or the old one. Trust the part of you that you're neglecting, not your vagina. If you're going to even consider getting involved with him, I suggest you learn from my many relationship mistakes," he proposed and I dismissed him as I ran towards Anderson whose clothes were drenched as he bobbed the baby who was suddenly cheerful up and down in the water and couldn't help but smile at her the more she laughed.

"Water weirdly calmed me down too as a kid, but do me favour and try not to cry too much for Viola because I heard about this big class assignment and it's usually done with a baby who has no proper home. And I want you to show her as much love as possible because maybe it can be the start of creating our home together. I've honestly never met anyone as complex as me before," he explained to the baby girl who was in nothing but a diaper and a pale pink T-shirt with a gold tiara on it. It made me think back to when Maddy practically told me I didn't need the title of queen to be one.

Anderson's charming words startled me as he was thinking as if a mirror didn't crash my life. The shirt on that child he already knew he wanted to raise with me before I was even a legal adult as I turned 18 the following day, made me think of what queen truly meant.

If someone took the time to analyze me as a queen, a ruler, they would come to the same conclusion I did. They would call me ruthless, a psycho, a motherfucking killing queen, one that used to be beautiful until blood followed her wherever she went. They'd say what appeared to be warm and fair quickly became cold and cruel alike my dark appearance after the shards of glass emotionally scarred me but vanished unlike they did in the body of an old love I destroyed.

They'd proclaim a life alone upon her, a life where she dances by herself with irons on her feet, killing her with any joy or happiness she felt despite the utter sorrow. This would be a life where Sophia lives with the man that made her happy and the evil queen would die a gruesome death by herself and see the hues of red and orange consuming her until nothing is left. That's the story most want to hear, the story that was portrayed in the media and in my head.

However, I am much more than a myth, the real thing and the average flawed human being, not a demon or a sorcerer. I might be damaged but still have feelings. It was then that I decided that in this new life, I was to try anything that tempted me within reason. If I was going to hell or destined for a gruesome death in the minds of others, I wasn't going to be something I wasn't on earth. I'm not evil, only trying to live, trying to survive but wanted to do much more than live. I desired to be the veil in evil, the woman living with all she deserved yet hiding her true face from all she didn't see as deemed to be in her life.

It was that thought alone that encouraged me to rush towards Anderson, not because I was horny but because I deserved to be loved by someone who understood innocence as I did.

Maddy shouted and swore for someone to calm the baby down who went by the name, Aliya, when considering she came from an abusive and toxic household, she needed a good change. Unfortunately, Maddy already viewed her like he viewed me, damaged, broken, shattered. However, Anderson on the other hand viewed her as someone who needed to feel a change of heart, a new start without being judged for it. I joined him, drenching myself in the water as he did and gently splashing them both with water, careful not to get any in the little one's hazel eyes with tints of orange in them, similar to my new eyes.

"You'll be a queen my little one but not in the royal kind of way or in the way where everyone likes you. You'll be hurt, betrayed, maybe almost raped, I hope not, but as long as you're happy with you, the rest of the world will come around, those meant to be in it for sure," I encouraged her as I held the palm of her milk chocolate hand within my own, feeling an immediate connection to her as I was her, alone and put in the hands of others to get by.

"When did you almost get raped? Did he..."

"No, he saved me when I was unconscious and can barely recall what happened. It was a game gone wrong that Anderson doesn't want to play anymore," I explained honestly to Maddy's desperate yell to look out for me that caused the sweet girl to cry bloody murder.

"I'm sorry people are such dicks as nobody should have to deal with that but I still don't trust this man!" Maddy voiced cruelly, projecting his voice loud and clear with each and every word.

"What do I have to do for you to trust me because I can at least be civil here! Viola isn't your sister you need to protect because she is too blinded and naïve to think for herself or your girlfriend, an acquaintance at most with how long you know each other for. That's the same in my case. Do I have to remove my jeans to show you my dick is smaller than yours so you feel you have the upper hand in this? Because you do; I need a place to stay and both partners to cooperate for this assignment," Anderson attempted to reason with Maddy.

"Fine. But I need this class to feel like at least my ethics can be right considering how I'm an orphan and all that holds me and my possessions are this boat. Viola needs this class to stand out for any universities involving Law. She wants to make things right for those people like in the town she grew up in who don't have voices. Why do you need this class and if you've been living in a classroom for so long, why a boat now?" Maddy questioned him in suspicion.

"I'll answer that once you tell me why you killed your parents," he ordered in a serious tone that left

Maddy looking stoned. In his attempt to conceal his emotions, he gave him a dirty look to turn the tables and make Anderson look stupid although it was obvious how out of it he seemed. "Dude, I'm screwing with you, just said that because you're an orphan," Anderson chuckled and Maddy awkwardly joined him.

"You can stay. I wasn't too sure if you were fucked in the head with that statement or not but I get your dark humour, I just want you and Viola sleeping in a different room when the baby isn't in this house and we don't have to take shifts," Maddy caved in as he desired to be as close to Anderson as possible to see what he was capable of, but not so close that it made him uncomfortable. Anderson attempted to calm the cranky little one that he handed to me when I lost hope and me whispering sweet lullabies in her ear as I did with Gloria's daughters for once didn't work. As we approached the boat, Maddy took her from me to give it a try and removed her saggy diaper in an instant as we entered the boat. He put it in the metal trash can by the front of the boat and removed her shirt he put in a hamper next to it. "She had fun but is obviously irritated that it was salt water she was in because when you threw her up and down in there, she likely swallowed some of the water and her stomach is upset. She needs to be all washed and then we'll help her remove some of her gas and feed her after. But I can wash her in a wash tub I have from when I thought I was having a baby while you two can wash up in my shower and I'm sure you have clothes and stuff back at the school, Andy, so just borrow anything of mine you'd like for now until you can retrieve that," Maddy explained, shocking us both by how calm he sounded and the words that came from him.

"There are two showers I'm assuming, right? Otherwise, we can take turns since we both smell like the sea," I asked Maddy while Anderson's eyes locked with my own, thinking the same thing as myself.

"There's only one and I catch fish for a living right now. It's not a very good living, so I want one shower, not two, so the water bill doesn't fly over the roof and I lose my boat. Please figure out a way to make it happen, remember I'm not asking for help with bills, just that you can pull your weight," he had guilt us and we nodded, heading down the wooden steps to the small room between Maddy's room and the old bedroom he mentioned I didn't take notice of before, probably because the bed that folded up on the wall wasn't much of a sight.

"So, two really short showers each and we can time each other or..."

"He's going to hear that it's two separate showers and I just want a place to live in with an actual bed and a chance to not wash the important parts in the bathroom sink," Anderson interrupted me and I nodded, understanding how much he desired a good change.

"Okay, I know you saw me in this state when you dressed me but this is a little different. I have weird broken heart markings you're going to have to ignore and am going to ask of you not to touch me like before if you can help it," I voiced to him and he stared me deeply in the eyes, allowing my heart to fall, but not shatter because he picked up the pieces and cared for it as if it was his own.

"I want you to feel safe with me. Whatever we see in there is only between us and nobody else. I already know so much about you without really knowing you and you deserve to know the same about me literally as you'll see my naked body and figuratively, what goes on in my head, in my life," he reassured me and began to remove his pale grey T-shirt with a sky-blue stripe down the middle and was going for his black shorts with a belt next when I was surprised his chest wasn't flat but had faint abs and a small shield of hair surrounding them. This shield went as far down as his belly button and as far up as his nipples that had muscle surrounding them. This was what I assumed despite the hair on his legs but I was proven wrong when the belt fell and so did his shorts and soon after his boxers were left on the ground with everything else. My eyes landed on the hair that continued past his belly button and what it was covering but my nerves and astonishment at the guy I assumed was a nerd with his baggy T-shirt and belt on his shorts, was hiding a lot. "Were you and the mirror man physical or is this sharing of water really weird? Am I the first man you're seeing like this?" He questioned me awkwardly as I still wasn't undressed.

"I'm sorry, you're not. I was kind of hoping you weren't more handsome under your clothes because Chance did a number on me, betraying me by pretending to love me and really loving Sophia the entire time. It's just hard to even strip down for another handsome man, one you already know you must have some sort of life with because it's all drawn out and that would be a waste," I opened up to him but hid feelings that were becoming much clearer to me, from him although I said it in a way that didn't take a genius to read between the lines.

"I can help you remove your clothes if that makes it easier. I know it's hard. The girlfriend that cleared out my hard-earned money a few months ago since I was stupid enough to give her access to that account if she ever needed it, is also in our summer school. I always fucking run into Lydia and she denies all she did, blames it on the bank even though since then, she'd always wear a different jewellery piece that looks expensive. We both can't get rid of our exes and unfortunately they were in our life to teach us stuff we needed to know for this moment. Chance taught you that you shouldn't convince someone to love you because that's not healthy and Lydia taught me that love alone can't make a relationship work. They served their purposes and it is difficult but dwelling on it, asking so many questions is pointless," he soothed me with his words and I lifted my arms up for him to help me remove my soggy jean coloured dress which he did quickly and gently before I removed my undergarments, leaving my wet clothes on top of his in front of the wooden door we closed before looking down as it was too much for me to acknowledge the way he was looking at me.

It was then that we entered the small, wooden shower with the white and navy striped curtains, across from the white toilet, left to the towel closet and right to the wooden sink with the white counter tops. We entered the curtains the light through the circular window brightened up, instantly located the shampoo, conditioner and body wash on the white floor of the shower with the wooden frame and Anderson gestured for me to back away as he turned the tap on, rotated it to warm and pushed the faucet so the shower head would squirt water our way. As I made my way closer to Anderson and the shower head, I tripped on an old shampoo bottle I didn't notice, yet wasn't given a chance to fall.

It was as if he could sense I was about to fall as I barely made any noise but he turned around in that moment and held my waist to prevent me from falling as he lifted me up as he stood in front of me, so tempting, wet and masculine. Our eyes locked like an ice-skating duo that were in sync with all movements as I trusted him not to drop me while our intimate moment lingered as he held me so strongly with my legs in the air. I wrapped my legs around him to feel a sense of comfort as he tried his best not to lose focus on the task at hand as he lathered us both as fast as he could while he stood under the shower head with me latched onto him.

"You're going quick because you're afraid you'll drop me or that we'll waste water?" I teased him as he continued the fast pace he was going at.

"I can hold you like this for maybe another minute based on some workouts I do here and there and Matt would kill us if we don't conserve water but neither are my focus right now," he paused to emphasis his next sentence that came out much slower and deeper than the rest of his speech. "I want you, all of you," he stated seductively and I bit down hard on my lip to avoid things from going any further. "I know it's fast and makes no sense but I want to do you on the bed that isn't Matt's because I can wow you more there and life is too short for crappy fucking and toxic relationships. I'll fuck you right and I promise to make you happy in all areas, pleasuring your body and mind," he explained rashly and I took the conditioner out of his hand to wash our hair even faster as we inhaled all the strong, minty smells of the spearmint scented products, our nostrils practically burning but not caring or even remembering Chance in that moment.

I'm sure it wasn't the heat of the water that made my cheeks flush as I even felt hot all over when he comforted me prior to the shower. The more he spoke, the more he proved his dull voice to be full of flavour, passion, lust, comfort, kindness, trustworthiness.

Anderson quickly bent down to release me from his legs once we both rinsed ourselves for the final time. The moment he turned the water off was the moment the curtains flew open in utter excitement as we rushed towards the cupboard to fetch a towel each after he helped me squeeze my hair out in the sink as well as finger comb it. After drying our bodies off with the teal, cotton towels, we dropped the towels as we had a good feeling Maddy was still upstairs and the old bedroom was just next door to the bathroom.

Anderson gestured for me to follow him closely behind in case Maddy was downstairs and we entered the old, almost empty room minus the bed attached to the violet coloured accent wall in a sky-blue room. I pushed the bed down, hearing it squeak, after Anderson shut the door. "It's dusty and old but will do the trick for sure," I stated as I blew off some dust along the comforter and pillows that were the same white and navy striped print as the shower curtains. I buried myself under them while Anderson left the room for a minute to return back with protection he stole from Maddy's room as he was smart that way.

Although, we were safely prepared, we talked a little prior, practically had the pillow talk before we began which dealt with any nerves since my last sexual encounter was with a man who didn't feel as strongly as I thought I did for him. "I wish your markings weren't broken because of Chance; I wish I could fill them," he stroked my jawline gently. "But your markings make you more beautiful to me, your entire story does because even though you killed and ran away from being queen, you are higher, more powerful than that. You have a confidence I really admire. I was told that you didn't hesitate to run away; you know how many times I almost tried to go back home and had to convince myself I was better than that, that I would find my own home. And then I met you and I think I now fully feel satisfied and without any regrets regarding not staying," Anderson voiced to me sweetly, touching me in a way nobody ever had.

I was always seen as the trapped girl attempting to find a way to escape and was now seen as the girl who didn't go back, the girl who started with nothing, was given all riches and was back to fending for herself because that felt like home to her.

Lying next to him naked oddly was the first time in my life I didn't feel the need to run back to being by myself because I knew from that day forward it would always be the two of us, just didn't understand the bigger picture of it all quite yet.

The Disturbing News

"It's funny you say that because I was basically told to run by my personal assistant who wanted me gone so she could be queen. I was taken away from my mom's corpse when she passed after birthing me, was taken away from my aunts to become queen against my own will, was taken away from a kingdom because of my murder and not being in the dark involving my home town I thought I could save and change for the better! I never fully chose what to leave, it either left me, like Chance, or I was told to leave it by force or better judgement," I confessed to him honestly while he gave me the most genuine stare in the world.

"You'll never have to leave me unless you want to," he said and the talking stopped as I practically pounced on him in that moment, claiming the home I never desired to leave.

"Stay here all day with me then," I moaned as we continuously were rolling and passionately making love, experimenting with every possible position we could think of. Anderson did voice to me that he wanted me to be comfortable and find things we both enjoyed. It was definitely a rollercoaster but we quickly got to a place where we knew what was best for us and went with it like two children playing their favourite game.

It wasn't necessarily aggressive, more so intense and soul consuming as we felt like one. It did however become more aggressive when the bed began to fold up halfway, forcing us to be on an arc-like angle but it didn't go fully back, allowing us to feel and be more adventurous without being squashed.

We both let out erupts of laughter that were silenced as I said softly, using my nickname for him when we're intimate, "Tommy, finish what you started and we can get off this old bed."

"Lola, my queen, you really thought I'd leave you without a finale?" he made my heart thump loudly with his lustful words alone that were put to an end when our lips embraced, our tongues practically overlapping each other's in a circular motion that reminded me of a ferris wheel that would be shown in a carnival scene of movies with a small town. Not to mention the fact that our bodies were practically in the air as we began to get super handsy again and fit like two pieces in a puzzle midair, free from all obstacles except for each other but that was overcame in our first day of meeting.

We slowed down the motions to truly savour it and because it was obvious we both desired more fun but were too drained as our breaths were heavy and heartbeats were fast the entire duration.

"Fuck working out," he teased as he attempted to pull a lever behind us to make the bed flat again.

"I never liked gym or running but this gives you a sweat and I think I could do you all day, but we have to go on a ferris wheel when we're not making love," I smiled at the sweet sentiment alone that I truly felt happy, so fast and so real.

"You say random things like that that confuse me as to how your mind thinks that has to do with the conversation at hand but does tell me to do just that with you. If I can see you smile like that, get into your head to understand your thoughts more and feel you more, that's good enough for me," he confessed sweetly while the lever he pulled pushed us further back. Yet it wasn't a complete inconvenience as we were pushed to the area the bed stood upon on the wall, close and cosy in a ball in pure darkness and only the soft breaths, voices and movements of one another could be felt.

"Well then, here's another random thing, this is a nice way to die all comfy under the covers next to you," I admitted calmly as I wrapped my arms around his neck and he did the same with my own as we rubbed each other's hickeys in our attempt to soothe the irritation.

"Best way to die but before that, we need a life together, so let's find the right lever to make that possible," he explained in a cute way as I quickly pecked his lips before opening a small drawer by the lever I opened to reveal coffee stained papers with red X's on them.

"Huh, Matt thinks he's a pirate," Anderson teased and we both shared a quick chuckle as he held it up through a hole on the side in the light and the maps were snatched out of his hand.

"I'm not a guy to think, one to know. Now don't go through things that don't apply to you and the button in the drawer opens the bed, acts as a good trap for intruders," he admitted a strange thought that made sense based on how he was dressed with Scarlet but I wasn't given a chance to inform Anderson when Maddy asked how we got in there. We proceeded by pulling the messy, loose, sand coloured sheets towards us so we'd be a little less embarrassed when we exited the wooden ledge.

When we managed to pull it towards us and cover ourselves in the sheets, I pushed the red button inside the drawer and the bed slowly came out as we faced Maddy.

"If you're a modern pirate, thief or whatever, you are more than fine with wasting water. You set us up, didn't you?" I came to a likely conclusion.

"I just encouraged a connection that was already there, didn't pressure anything. But I bathed Aliya and made a little cot for her to sleep in and when she's awake she's all yours to deal with. I have a workout to perfect to teach the teacher as our first assignment tomorrow and have a date. I should be back in a few hours but if I'm not, microwave meals are in the fridge and I'll be back before the day is over," he said much less than what was actually going on, didn't even wait for us to get dressed and check on Aliya, just grabbed a duffle bag with a tuxedo in it and cement grey, sweat material, drawstring shorts. He gave us a peace sign before leaving rather suddenly, surprising us both as we didn't question him and only said goodbye to be polite.

"What the fuck was that about?" I asked Anderson as he knew Maddy better than I did.

"Probably one of two things if not both. The baby was too much for him and he didn't think you'd sleep with me. He was trying to convince himself he'd want a child again one day, be part of the future we drew out, but it's too hard for him to get past and the shower thing was a test for you to see how you see him. He was horrible at playing the games others wrote out for him, dares and even worse at truths but blocking people out and making his own game where he had others exactly where he wanted them is what he has a talent in. That tux is for the date of my sister's dreams, a fancy dinner with ballroom dancing, the prom she never had because our parents didn't want her to lose her virginity, they saw that day in particular as an excuse for it. She did them one better and almost had a baby the year after," he rolled his eyes. "They never had real dates but since Matt sees that a girl that is as genuine and insightful as yourself chose a nobody like me, he's actually trying with her, being a good man for a change and when you fall for that crap, he will be over his little obsession by then," Anderson warned me in utter frustration.

"And what makes you so sure I'd fall for that crap? What makes you so sure I like the feeling of being used that I'd let another guy do just that?" I asked him rhetorically. "I'm smarter than you may think and I can promise you even if he has a tendency of being soft around me, a little different than other girls, we'd want two different things. I'll always want a relationship that makes you feel like the main character. But having sex and being in a committed relationship are two different things…"

"We had sex," Anderson cut me off.

"Yeah, and for the first time in a long time, I felt like it was my own life I was living. For once I wasn't dragging my feet along in someone else's. Maddy could never give me that," I admitted, accidentally slipping in the nickname I had for him. "Matty was what I meant to say," I quickly recovered myself.

"I know his first name is Madison and that wasn't the first time you accidentally slipped the nickname; I am involved enough in the world to know who he is. I find Law interesting, am super invested in it but couldn't do it as a career, too stressful. I like to do it on my own and feel like my own boss," he explained and I nodded, understanding exactly where he was coming from.

"You easily have what it takes to be a lawyer after putting the pieces together of a tough case from Boston but know you'll be the bad guy in someone's eyes and only want to do good, want to build," I added as I made my way outside the nearly empty bedroom, my bare feet grazing the cold, wooden flooring as I undid my suitcase to grab clean undergarments and Anderson began to also change.

"Sometimes you have to be bad to do good, but the thing is that I enjoy rules so much, law, crime, right versus wrong, ethics, that I'd be stupid to turn it into work. It would take the fun out of it, make me miserable," Anderson brought up a point that never crossed my mind.

"That's fair but it could also be the best thing for you, doing what you love every day of your life," I smiled just with the thought of being a lawyer, fighting for justice, what is right.

"So many marriages fail and they are with who they love every day, so tell me how you know if anything will last? All you can do is create a plan and hope it carries through," he threw on Maddy's clothes but sounded nothing like him. Maddy may have had intentions I disagreed with at the time but at least he could take a leap when he desired to and not always stand around in hopes of his dreams finding him.

"I don't know for certain if I'll stop loving justice but what I do know is that I love it now, so why waste my time doing anything else other than that?" I added honestly as I was about to grab clean undergarments from my metal suitcase near the racks of women's clothes to find the photo moved from near Maddy's bed into there with the corner folded over as if to draw my attention to the back of it.

Queen you were, good you aren't. You weren't very nice, otherwise I'd let you out for a price. But what I will do is tell you to watch the news and don't forget that the game never stops no matter what anyone says.

I almost passed out at the sight of the threatening yet slightly poetic words on the back of a traumatic picture. My entire body stood still as Anderson helped me into my pale grey undergarments that lacked diamonds but were made out of satin and consisted of lace trims with emeralds on the bow on both the bra and underwear.

He delicately stroked my body the moment he saw me not dressed and instantly caught my distress when he brought an outfit of Maddy's to the hallway to quickly throw on. As my body loosened up and became less tense, Anderson slipped a strapless, neon orange coloured dress on me and carried me towards Maddy's water bed he laid me on. He positioned his body near my own despite the flowy movement of the bed so that I could lean my head on his lap as he played the news as the note with the neatest handwriting I've ever seen instructed us to do which I informed him when he comforted me.

"The palace by Edgebrook has declared princess Sophia is alive and well, for no heart can physically beat for another human being but when attempted will collapse. She is currently in hospice but the queen's location is noted but not what she looks like. Evil acts change a person's core along with their outsides. King Liam desires the creature be put behind bars for the trauma inflicted on his daughter he didn't realize could love a man hardly anyone knew as well as Sophia Wilington and Viola Wilington. Viola unlike the prophecy wasn't ended by Sophia but ended the life of the man in the mirror, Chance Nosredna. Someone in the school she is at has their theories about her and will come back with her. The king's man on the job backed out but the police have even better people and are on it. Everyone encourages you to just turn yourself in, Viola, it would make things much easier, especially considering the nearest city to your little town has a large prison with the sentence of the death penalty as the highest charge for murder," the news reporter started off stating the facts but added her own personal opinion in there before the reporter changed from the judgemental red head middle-aged woman to a perky, blonde young reporter who was doing the weather forecast.

"Turn it off! I have a lot to deal with because you weren't only hired, someone else in this school was. My assistant from the palace, Gloria, likely sent me to this school with a plan for me to be put behind bars or dead so she could become queen without anyone stopping her and didn't have the guts to backstab me in front of me. And Liam did let me go that day, understood how betrayed I felt by him not giving me the authority I deserved and thought I had but why hire someone if he knew what I looked like and where I was going? Unless he still saw me as the girl he married, still saw me as the light blonde with the peach skin because he found it difficult to completely see me as evil while I'm thinking Gloria saw an in between since I helped out with her kids so much and was there for her when she pretended to be sad about uh Matt's death she pretended happened since they were involved a long time ago," I admitted to him honestly and looked down at the neon orange strapless dress he put me in and laughed at how strange my pale grey bra straps looked in it but I wore the dress like that because he was afraid the top part would slip down if I left the house.

"Look at me, Viola, and listen," he said reassuringly as he put his hand on my shoulders where the pale grey straps laid. "You aren't dying or going to jail with me by your side because we're going to find whoever is looking for you and get them off your tail and that means you have to be yourself. Just pretend you saw nothing and aren't being looked for. I have my suspicions, being really into Law and all and from what you're telling me, Matt might not be working for the police but has something to do with this or knows more than we think based on the fact that a woman who wanted to take your spot as queen is connected to the man whose boat you're currently living on. I'll watch Aliya and I want you to go on a walk, get some air and do any homework later because you deserve a little mental break and I can't picture a six month old lasting very long outside," he looked out for me and slightly startled me regarding Maddy yet I couldn't picture it although it was the most logical based on all I discovered so far.

However, logic was never a huge part of my life with deceit, betrayal, heartache and backstabbing constantly taking over my entirety. I found it difficult to trust someone immediately but felt a kind of connection with both men, different connections yet sort of similar as I didn't feel alone in different aspects with both of them, and didn't desire to go back to feeling so empty.

I desired a genuine connection with them despite my hesitation with particular attributes both displayed like the streak outside of the lines wasn't the full picture but didn't make it any less beautiful in my opinion. I should've been more careful, should've kept my distance and caution because of the streak, not gone after Maddy. Maddy was logically my ticket to feeling trapped yet again. Doing that was just the beginning to creating my own trap of relying on those who would never do anything for you unless there was something in it for them.

Someone To Understand Me

I left the boat with the intention to look for Maddy and took the traumatic photo with me I wished I could remember exactly what happened.

I strolled along the dirt path of the school that led into a forest which was full of blinding sunlight as the trees barely covered it. I followed the path, waiting to hear some kind of water running or special water scenery as Maddy seemed to be drawn to it with his water bed and the fact that he was living on a boat.

I didn't know exactly where I was going, only happened to walk for a good ten-minutes, follow my instincts and find Maddy sitting on a rocky edge that overlooked aqua blue water down below.

"What are you doing here? Shouldn't you be playing house with Anderson?" he sensed my presence and added a snarky remark before I could even answer him.

"I'm here because I care what happens to you and I wanted you to tell me if you recognize the handwriting. Looks like it's probably a woman's with how small and neat it is and you slept with a lot of women from school," I voiced to him honestly as his ocean eyes suddenly went dark as he reached for the picture but had yet to lay his eyes on the front.

"This has to be one sick ass joke, right?" he yelled, sounding beyond aggravated. His face practically fell as he analyzed the writing.

"What's wrong? Do you know who wrote it?" I asked him eagerly.

"Yeah, I kind of lived in her for nine months and had to exit her pussy to come into this cruel world," Maddy explained in a blunt manner as he stood by the cliff, looking down at it, considering the possibility of ending it all until I rushed over to him and pulled him away with all my might.

"I don't know how she would be alive or why she would hide it from you and why she'd be taunting me but what I do know is that you have a lot to offer this world. The world deserves to know Madison Chambers and how tough he is despite the bad relationship he was in, the child he didn't physically get, the broken childhood and blood on his hands, one that he wasn't solely responsible. So, don't leave it before others get a chance to know why you were put here and it wasn't just to protect people like me that felt alone our entire lives or didn't expect anything different to happen than before," I confessed to him and he turned his face towards me, pushing me away from the cliffside as he let out a few deep breaths before doing something reckless.

His glistening ocean blue eyes sank deep into my own, allowing my heart to feel his heavy and strong beats as I attempted to hug him for comfort. Maddy brushed me away enough to grasp his hands around the sides of my face where he planted a kiss on my lips words could not even come to describe. I didn't kiss him back and that was when he got the hint to stop but that didn't make it mean any less.

When Maddy's lips touched my own, I could taste the cigarette residue he probably inhaled shortly after he left the house, feel the hard and chapped indents in his lips that likely were bleeding prior if not close to bleeding. I felt the few tears that managed to escape down his cheeks with everything that was tough for him to process and his mid-length, straight for the most part despite the wavy ends of his shaggy, dirty blonde hair with walnut coloured roots brush against my neck as sweaty as could be. I was able to feel all he went through as if it was on me except it wasn't and I was with Anderson, so it didn't matter how real things felt, especially with what he said after I tried to talk to him about it.

Then there were his intense eyes, nose that slightly scrunched when around me, nervous ticks full of emotion that screamed commitment, yet he could never give himself that, didn't think he was ready because like me, he never had a constant in life. His parents both died like mine, or we think his dad did at least, and we both felt at fault for their deaths. With Harmony miscarrying his child a while back, he likely felt as if like me who killed my own boyfriend with the glass that he lived in after he hurt me so much, that he was destined to be by himself, have flings at most and nothing meaningful that could crash down on him or that he could kill like his dad.

"Hey, um, I know things between Anderson and I are super fresh but I do feel the need to tell him about us..."

"I'm going to cut you off there because there isn't an us. I don't even know why I took your advice with trying to date Harmony. I made it obvious to you that I don't date but if you want to end things with Andy, find a different reason since him and I already don't get along," Maddy explained coldly.

"I'm still telling him about the kiss..."

"Did fucking with him make you suddenly think you're in love with him because you barely know the guy," he interrupted me cruelly.

"Well, turn the photo over. He saved me from whatever bad incident almost occurred, he's showing me a future that offers commitment and love, and he did me so fucking good! He stays during tough moments unlike someone I know, so I can say I know him well enough to say there's a future," I rubbed his absence at times in his face and he increased the distance between us until he ran towards the ledge of the rocky cliff and jumped, leaving the picture behind along the edge.

I did what any good friend would do. Mad or not at his foolish mistakes, I strangely didn't desire for him to go through whatever it was he was, alone.

I let my beige flip-flops slip off, the rough, crumply grey and brown rocks along the edge of the cliff toughen my feet like the sand paper my insides had become. I didn't even bother to look down, wasn't scared or hesitant, just jumped but instantly regretted it when I practically flew towards the body of water below and the life that flashed before my eyes was full of blood. My entire life was a bloodbath, torture, betrayal and full of backstab. Love wasn't felt for very long and most of it wasn't real.

My body splashed deep under the brisk water, but as usual, I managed to bring myself back up, stronger than the flow of the sea that was pushing me down. I didn't even have to search for Maddy as I heard him shrieking, "Woo hoo!" several times as I held my nose while I breathed in my attempt to unplug my water filled ears. It thankfully worked by the second breath.

"I just wanted to feel a little free before taking your advice with Harmony. It might not be something I'm used to but maybe I want a baby of my own one day. But I think someone cares about me enough to jump down with me. What if I was trying to kill myself? Would you have literally just died with me?" he voiced to me very serious words I could barely comprehend.

"I don't know but what I do know is I'm loving you until you can love yourself because protecting yourself from getting hurt isn't love. I know it's hard, but you need to open yourself up to getting hurt because there will always be that risk but if you don't risk it, you'll never be happy," I admitted to him honestly as he brushed the front pieces of my wet hair behind my ears and kissed me yet again, except this kiss was much different than the first.

Instead of his lips allowing me to feel all that made him who he was, they said goodbye with the way they exploded like fireworks full of wonder.

"It won't happen again because I did have an idea to surprise Harmony and I'm doing that for me not because of anything you said," Maddy lied and I saw right through it. I saw right through his clear, blue eyes and his perfect, unforgettable kiss.

"I care for you because you gave me a home and didn't need to know my story to do that, just did. And you wanted me to remember that, not as a goodbye but a definite see you around in more ways than one. You definitely have game, just use it on someone who's open to it," I suggested to him with a backhanded compliment that had many kind words behind it.

"Fine. I'll start treating you like a sister if you don't tell Anderson a thing about the kisses because it's only me getting a little horny and nothing meaningful or worth changing any dynamic for," he proposed a devious idea he held his hand out for me to shake and got much more than he was bargaining for when he gave me a friendly kiss along my cheek, close to my lips but not on them.

With this action, I felt a sudden shock that made him back away from me. To our utter astonishment, the marking Chance left by my lip vanished for good. I didn't quite understand why, only that we weren't meant to live a life without each other, complicated or not. And we did plan to find out how his mom was connected to all of this or if someone was playing a terrible joke on us.

Maddy pulled apart from me and said, "If you're going to love me until I understand risk is the path to happiness, then I'm going to save you from your risks that weren't worth it, going to be the body you lean on half naked and feel nothing other than warmth," he chuckled while splashing me with the refreshing water until we made our way to a rocky edge of the small, secluded sea and walked up the rocky steps we didn't take notice of as we made our way to the top.

I held the photograph from before that had an envelope underneath and opened it to reveal a photo of Maddy kissing me, but it wasn't blackmail which surprised me.

Madison,

I know I screwed up. I know I left you when things were hard but you look so happy without me that it makes it hard to come back. You probably don't even want me to come back. But I will tell you this, I saw what happened to that girl's marking that will make her even less recognizable. She's dangerous and not just because she killed someone I'll tell you more about another time but because anyone she gets close to dies. First her mom, then her aunts she was lied to about them being asleep to gain her trust, then her first boyfriend and I know you're next. Sophia was destined to be the end of her. Not the king's daughter but the name in general which means wisdom. She's too smart in every situation she's put it that she survives it but those close to her don't. I have my reasons for leaving you but am not doing that twice and want you to follow my voice, Madison.

With love,

Mom

"I think I'll be moving out, maybe can sell the diamonds or other gems on my undergarments for rent. I'd be away from both you and Anderson and I'd still physically be free," I said glumly yet was strong as I always have been and left everything there for him as I began to walk away, towards the boat to grab my things and go.

"If you leave, you're doing what my mother wants! You're giving in and are telling her that your wisdom is getting to you, leaving you all by yourself and I still need to understand love and you're the only one who can do that; y mom would understand," he sighed as his words allowed my stomach to find all the knots that ever laid place in them and slowly began to untangle themselves, feeling the good I never could feel all at once.

"Fine but I need to know more about your mom, if she has any connections at this summer school because my life is literally on the line. I need to know what I'm up against!" I exclaimed to him sternly.

"We need to go to a cemetery first and go from there," Maddy breathed heavily.

"But how could someone fake your mom's handwriting? Why is the real question?" I asked him confused.

"To remove me from the situation by pretending to be my mom, pretending to be sorry for the pain she caused I blamed myself for," he replied glumly.

"What if Anderson and I start interviewing other students to see if any have relations to your mom or have strong opinions regarding me murdering

Chance and you can deal with the burial stuff and we can meet in the middle," I suggested.

"That's not a terrible idea except for the fact that you're not going to be focused on the suspects with Andy. I don't even know why you slept with him so quickly anyway; I thought you were better than me," Maddy explained kindly, emphasizing the last part.

"I might not always be as wise as the prophecy says but at least I can say that I love myself," I held back the bloody tears that I could feel were on the verge from tumbling down my cheeks.

"Having sex with a guy the same day you don't trust him at first, the same day you meet him is loving yourself?" Maddy irritated me with his question as he had a habit of doing.

"Yes. With Chance, I didn't find a way to have sex with him for almost two years and I got hurt. I've learned that waiting doesn't matter because sometimes you need to just go for things you don't think you can do again but do anyways to prove yourself wrong. And to add to this, Anderson made me feel and understand belonging and courage so quick in a way I never had before," I voiced to Maddy honestly, taking in his orbs that made the sea look so bright in that moment.

"Just be careful, okay. Your heart can only handle so much and keep in mind, protection can only do so much, I know that from experience. Now, if you excuse me, I am going to give Harmony a real date and accidentally grabbed shorts instead of a towel, so I'll be using those to dry off. Are you okay to go home?" he looked out for me while a frightening thought came to mind when he mentioned protection.

"Dumb question, I never used protection with Chance since he was kind of trapped in the mirror despite it projecting his body, didn't have to. But Anderson kind of took some from your room, they weren't expired or anything were they?" I asked Maddy curiously and he looked at me with wide eyes.

"By some, do you mean you used one each?" he confirmed and I nodded.

"That's a huge misconception, less is more. Both rubbing against each other could make one fall off easier and the ones I keep out have small holes in them. I blame that for the reason why Harmony and I have a baby up above. The baby wouldn't have been conceived if it wasn't for that bad box, kept it as a memory. The actual condoms are in the back of my underwear drawer," he explained and my stomach dropped at that thought.

"Some people rely on the pull-out game and never get pregnant or some get so caught up in the moment that they forget to protect themselves and still don't get knocked up, or who knows, you could be infertile. Watch the baby with Andy tonight and I have connections back home who will deal with my mom's grave and we'll start our interviews tomorrow. See how you feel and I'll grab you a pill from the drug store to prevent a pregnancy just in case," Maddy reassured me as usual which was unexpected yet felt right.

"Thanks, have fun and take risks with Harmony tonight," I added kindly and left Maddy with the evidence since it was his mom's handwriting.

Maddy had a habit of not being there when I appeared most vulnerable, like being exposed on the concrete while someone attempted to rape me. Instead of pushing Anderson and I apart, he brought us towards each other and led me towards a vulnerable situation I felt seen in. When I called his name as loud as I could, screamed and cried, in my head of course, he was never there. But when I expected to be on my own, there he was pushing his flavour of the day aside to give me a home, pushing me towards what he saw was good for me and always having my back.

As I rightfully assumed, Madison Chambers was a protector. He wasn't some knight in shining armour that was always standing in front of me but the kind of guy who pushed his interests aside for the better good, the kind of guy who I caught watching me through the bushes and trees as he followed me to the boat to ensure I arrived safely.

If I was a lover and Maddy was a protector? What did that make Anderson?

Someone who didn't feel the need to protect me or necessarily love me just yet but someone who understood me, someone I could constantly feel when he wasn't there. What is the name for that?

Maddy would say a traitor as he trusted Anderson as much as he trusted him but I think a hero is what he was. His ethics behind his actions always went by logic and although he was interested in me, it was obvious he was just as intrigued by my case, in me obtaining my justice for Chance's wrongdoings. I had yet to turn 18 and felt as if I lived long enough to turn into a villain in the eyes of others but I will always feel like a victim. My words and feelings were pushed away from me, weren't seen because of one rash action and that's why I'm not the main character in my own story.

I headed towards the boat that day thinking I was, thinking I had control over my own actions, my own results, consequences and rewards. However, in actuality, many of my own actions were dictated or influenced by the response of others or how they were situated. In that case, I would always be the bad guy, evil, the villain in someone else's story because in comparison to those who are heroes, it would be hard to root for me.

Despite this, our plan to discover who was truly onto me conspired the following day which happened to be my 18th birthday when the realms of bad and good blurred. I may have been oblivious to it at the time but some people will always see me for my crime and my past. It isn't those people that will be my downfall but myself if I don't remember the simple moments with good company until the realms become more clear, more distinct and distant in comparison to one another.

Monsters Don't Get Love

Parenting a child at our young age was a lot to handle and our little Law project gave us a taste of that, a taste of what could've been. Could Anderson and I have conceived a child? I'll never know the answer to that because I did take the medication Maddy brought me and never found out.

One might say it's better I don't know the entire truth, think of another possible scenario, one where I didn't get exactly what one believed I deserved. However, I feel as if a different way of feeling trapped would've done me well. It would've been similar to how the end began for me as it would be the idea of feeling trapped with a loophole except it would've felt more real than that. I would've felt like I was the part of a real family. Although it would've been nothing other than a mere illusion, it would've been nice.

A young woman, a teen mom I could've been in a house Anderson and I built together, studying Law virtually while he worked construction outside our house. There could've been long talks as we struggled to calm down our cranky baby boy who was the spitting image of his dad with those rare sterling grey eyes that could make any cloudy day not feel miserable. There could've been smiles exchanged and hearts constantly thumping at the idea that we'd never be helpless or alone without each other.

There'd be stories shared with details we never heard the first several times that would bind us all the further. I would've likely convinced him to get a vasectomy because one child was more than enough for us to handle together, especially so young and he would've agreed because as long as I'm happy, he is. That was our entire dynamic and I never questioned it because I believed that the world will give you back the good you put into it. How stupid was I?

Instead, I found myself on a boat with Anderson taking care of a child that wasn't ours but could've been, another thing that was unfortunately dismissed. This was another opportunity to be apart of the perfect family, a place of belonging when glancing at it in a mirror but not deep into the depths of his heart, mind and soul. I made my fair share of mistakes too like everything regarding Maddy I hid from him but he took the win home.

"Did it rain or something?" Anderson questioned me the moment his eyes met mine as I entered the boat and saw him on the leather sofa with his feet out and Aliya asleep on his light grey V-neck shirt that was covered in drool and spit up, some dry and some not.

"It doesn't matter but I did figure out whose writing is on the letter or whose writing someone at our summer school is attempting to mimic," I tried my hardest not to smile but it was difficult. The faint smile I unintentionally snuck in was for my moment with

Maddy in the water, not because I was closer to being free, living a brand-new life free from baggage, free from weight.

"Your efforts really paid off. I would ask you how but I have a feeling I won't like the answer, so just tell me what you found out and what we have to do next," Anderson asked me kindly and in a warm, comforting voice to not wake up the sleeping baby.

"You're right because I did speak to who you believe is the enemy but it led me to find out that the writing belongs to his dead mom who is either alive or someone wants to taunt Maddy by mocking his mom's handwriting," I admitted to him and his eyes narrowed, disagreeing on the only thing we ever fought about, my relationship with Maddy.

"Okay, I've fought my entire life and am not going to bother saying how you shouldn't have spoken to him about this. He lives with us. I expected you to tell him some of this eventually, not this quick but what's done is done. What I do know is Madison's case and I know all of his mom's connections, so if the writing is hers, I know exactly who to start with," he stated confidentially.

"Tell me what you know then. Maddy is investigating if his mom is actually dead or not but taking notes on our suspicions can help us tomorrow," I stated as I fetched a notebook from the drawer of a wooden shelf by the couch which was a lucky guess and fetched the black inked pen attached to it to write in it but when grabbing the notebook, more pictures fell out of the notebook with the sand coloured cover.

Pictures of Chance and I gazing at each other in the mirror when I looked like my old, innocent self fell out of the notebook. Maybe Maddy wasn't fully on our side. I used the fury those photos and the one hiding them brought upon me and asked Anderson everything he knew to put down a timetable and figure out who Maddy's mom had a connection with at our school besides Maddy.

"So, that's you?" Anderson asked in awe as he took the photos out of the notebook to glance at them more closely and couldn't help but grin at them without any teeth but just as much joy.

"You can tell? I don't recognize that girl at all. I may have only looked like that this morning but it feels like forever. I feel like time stood still when my entire body was as shattered as the mirror and the glass barely pricked me because I was inhumane, my actions were inhumane..."

"You mean killing Chance intentionally when he chose princess Sophia over you or the guilt associated with it all?" Anderson asked, appearing to be disappointed in my action yet understanding at the same time.

"Both. That girl is just so foreign and the shards of glass made me look so much older, almost become a woman, just not the pure kind," I sighed and he held my hand tightly, stroking the tips of his fingers against my knuckles.

"Your choices don't make you good or bad but who you are. They add character to you and show you that doors like that can stay closed and still make you who you are. I can tell that girl is you because in these photos compared to now, your eyes never changed. The colour changed but not the depth behind them. Even before killing Chance Nosredna, you lacked innocence in your light eyes, they have a tint of brown in the angles in the photos. Your action just allowed that brown to show more. Brown is usually a gross, hideous, ugly colour. My eye colour is naturally brown. I wear grey contacts to make them more rare, not so ordinary. I left my brown eyes back with my old life. I'd constantly stare at them in the mirror as tears would leave them when my mom would belittle my worth, Bs weren't good enough in school and even As weren't that great if someone had an A+. It got so bad that I'd change my grades on tests and even make my own report cards but they caught on and my dad would beat me for that. My parents were super old fashioned and as a man, I needed a good career, in medicine which was preferred to support my future wife and kids. It became a lot, so I took off, wanted to take Harmony with me who didn't have that pressure but doesn't have a great relationship with food since my mom told her that a handsome man doesn't go for average or plus sized women. It was super fucked up but those terrible eyes I left behind found me again, except they aren't so terrible. Your eyes tell me that I'm not alone and the orange specks that are hidden within the brown remind me of the sunshine, the warm rays that hit my forehead as I ran with nothing other than the possessions in my school backpack at the age of 12 and didn't go home that day because it wasn't home. The streets were more of a home than that house but enough of me rambling," he paused for a moment to truly highlight his point. "My point is that my brown eyes always said pain, helplessness or loneliness but looking into yours, feeling your body warmth without feeling your body makes me completely re-evaluate what brown meant to me. Brown is beautiful. Just like dirt that supports living organisms, brown keeps me going and I think I'm starting to see where I came from as less than a burden because I wouldn't be standing with eyes that have probably seen as much as mine," he comforted me as he removed his contacts to show me the hazel brown eyes that were slightly lighter than my own but had seen just as much, if not more and were astonishing. He forced me to re-evaluate what brown eyes mean and make me feel.

His words alone took me to a place of safety, a place that wasn't stationary because for the first time, it would travel with me. If him opening up wasn't enough, him removing my dress after removing his soft hand from my own and wrapping me in the cream, knit blanket on the couch to feel warm, was reassurance enough that he cared.

"I don't feel alone for the first time in a while which is probably strange considering how quick things are going. I'm sorry you had to deal with all that and you leaving was just as strong as Harmony staying, both take just as much courage," I replied kindly and his eyes that felt much more close, in ways I didn't even have a clue about yet, lit up by my response.

"Time isn't anything special. An hour can feel like a year with the wrong person and a year can feel like an hour full of the best things imaginable with the right one. And this day can feel like an entire life with the feelings and similarities we already exposed. You're right but I am happy she finally moved out last year and am happy we reconnected at this school," he couldn't have described my emotions and lack of sense of time any more clearly.

"I know her and Maddy have been on and off, but at this point, why aren't they just living together?" I asked him in hopes of slowly removing someone I thought of as a friend away from us.

"It's better they don't because that's commitment at its finest and I can't picture him giving her that," he voiced to me and my stomach dropped at that big word, thinking back to Maddy kissing me not once but twice on the lips and once close to the lips, and how it made me feel.

"Yeah, but is it even a good idea for us to live on the boat with him? Like was he even telling the truth about that being his mom's handwriting?" I asked Anderson in frustration regarding nothing ever staying the same or being two-dimensional.

He tapped his hand on the leather sofa cushion for me to sit next to him on the couch as he didn't want to wake Aliya and I did just that, leaning my head on his shoulder as he twirled the tiny pieces of hair behind my ears with his free hand.

"I don't know but if he is, there are three people at our summer school that would easily have motive. Matt's brother he claimed to have stolen his girlfriend and life might not be on good terms with him but was a good con man, had a criminal record and would easily mimic his mom's handwriting to make Matt uncomfortable or could be in on it with him to throw you off guard, maybe they patched things up. He could easily pass as a summer school student if he wanted to be responsible for your arrest. Maybe he wants to prove to himself he's a good person or maybe Matt's guilt has finally ate him up and he wants to turn himself in and get less jail time by turning you in..."

"Forget about Maddy and his brother, Olie. Who else?" I shouted and the baby slightly squirmed on Anderson's chest but the way his arm supported her and stroked her back as she laid on the shoulder I wasn't lying my head on, stopped her from waking up or crying.

"Uh, there's Caroline Martinas, Matt's mom's best friend's daughter who is a year younger than us. She's a goodie two shoes and because of that, she's stuck on what to put in her college essay to make her stand out, so she's taking some extra classes in the summer to stall for time. And there's anyone in Law-related classes that would be intrigued by the case, but that's broader. Matt or his brother are highly likely and Caroline is like a close second," Anderson stated the cold, hard, gruesome facts to me as I stared at him in disbelief.

I wasn't Scarlet but was still invited on his boat with open arms, was still held, still looked after, still kissed, still treated like a friend with a touch of something else that could've been romantic yet still felt rather foreign to me.

He was in the right place at the right time. He gave me a home when I felt like I was in as many pieces as the shattered mirror itself. He made me feel heard in a way Chance couldn't. Chance was physically trapped like me but didn't understand it mentally. Maddy did and by letting that similarity fog my judgment, I realized friends never existed for me.

My only constant was myself and even that was a lie with how over the place and consumed with thoughts, ideas and energy, much not belonging to me, I was. My entire body ached as if it was malnourished like most of my childhood. Yet this time being malnourished was different. I had my necessities but lost my trust and faith completely in people as a whole. That wasn't including Anderson who didn't feel like another person but a soul mine always laid beside or wondered about in times of sorrow.

Anderson was the only person I held onto at the time and didn't think twice about doing so because he knew enough about my past and instead of destroying me, chose to help me. It didn't make much sense for him to throw aside his duty to the king unless he really did care for me and wanted me to not feel lonely when he had nobody to talk to or turn to when he ran away from home.

"Can we start interviewing the girl you mentioned before Maddy gets back?" I asked Anderson anxiously as a genius look appeared on his face. His hazel brown eyes grew brighter as a brilliant idea came upon him.

"If you know anything about policing, it's that you go undercover because people can easily lie their way through interviews but it's harder during genuine connection. You need to get that girl to become your best friend," he proposed an idea I didn't agree with as I didn't believe in using people like pawns in a game.

"Is there another idea where the girl doesn't feel betrayed…"

"That's what you'll feel like if you don't go through this. She could be the one out to put you behind bars or end your life…"

"She also might not be…," I interrupted him as he did with me.

"But she could be," he protested. "She could literally end your life," he added, putting me in full survival mode by using those words alone.

"How do I go about being someone's best friend when I never even had one that stayed?" I asked him glumly, the lumps in my stomach still not supporting liking his idea.

"You be all you ever thought was missing in your connections. Be what I am to you but for you. Care for her in a way where you actually befriend her, so if it's not her out to get you, you did nothing wrong," he attempted to make me see things differently yet I couldn't.

"And if she is out to put me behind bars, I used her to get the upper hand in things. I'd be just as bad as Chance," I confessed to him and he shook his head.

"No, Chance did what he did for personal reasons but you'd be doing this for justice of what he did to you. It's just something to think about," he attempted to persuade me but failed.

"Do you know why I killed Chance? Why I really killed him?" I emphasized the second question as I deeply gazed into Anderson's eyes that had the same loneliness mine did.

"Because he loved Sophia, not you," he recklessly blurted out yet it didn't sting as much as I thought since that wasn't the complete truth.

"Ow, blunt much," I teased, gently whacking his side in a joking manner and he slightly chuckled between a half ass apology. "Seriously though, I killed what I desperately wanted out of the fear of never having that again. I didn't deserve what it was I felt with Chance, real or not and I don't deserve you, whatever the fuck this is between us. Any connection I made betrayed me and I just know that everyone hates me without even knowing me. I was born without parents and although my aunts thankfully stepped in, I feel like I was just lucky, that I was meant to never have a support system that exceeded me. Whatever this is between us isn't real because if you betrayed me, I don't think I'd even have it in me to kill you," I muttered as he planted a gentle kiss on my cheek.

"Just because you can't kill someone, doesn't mean you don't feel connected to them," he stated as I pictured the shard of glass grazing my heart instead of his and wasn't too sure what that meant and didn't desire to startle him with that gruesome image.

"Yeah, I don't know. Is there any other way we can begin our mission to find out who is onto me?" I suggested.

"Hey, Caroline! Come on the boat for a good ten, I know where Matt keeps his stash of booze!" Anderson projected his voice, going against my better judgment and left me with a crying baby to deal with he woke up by his screaming as our suspect approached the boat.

"Carry is fine and I haven't been on this boat in forever. Maybe since a few months back when I was here literally every day. Probably for the best since I always forgot my clothes here or had them ripped off. That dress on the ground is actually mine," the bubbly girl with caramel coloured skin, a faint Indian accent, charcoal grey, semi-circle framed glasses and short, curly and brownie coloured hair that landed at the top of her ears stated.

"That and rumour has it that Matt turned you gay," Anderson teased her and her cheeks tinted pink.

"It took fucking him for a good three months for dumb me to realize that," she mocked Anderson's choice of words.

"I think I like you. I would've told him off too and I slept with Anderson and think I'm sort of dating him," I chimed in, not to solve the mystery of who is the mole at school but to not necessarily have a good life but a fun moment.

"You're funny, blanket girl," we both laughed as she gestured towards my blanket dress that I was shocked held up, only being tucked into my bra and all as I rocked Aliya to soothe her. "Honestly, I always knew, just wasn't willing to admit it until the most popular guy in school barely made me feel horny and I was forced to admit it," she shrugged.

"I'm glad you're open about it now," I replied with a faint smile.

"Me too," her sigh was full of relief. "But I didn't come back in this boat to play games or drink booze I already know the hiding spot of. I know you're new here, blanket girl, and Anderson could use a better group of friends. I'm having a party tonight and wanted to invite you both and Matt if he's around. He may not have been the boyfriend I needed but was understanding and surprisingly listened more than he spoke," she explained with a slight laugh, handing us a bright orange invite and then taking off as fast as she arrived.

"Thanks so much but we have an actual baby to take care of thanks to Law class and I don't think…," I began to say until Anderson interrupted me as usual.

"We'll find a way to be there even if it isn't for long," he added just when she left.

"See you both there then," Carry exclaimed in excitement with her turquoise brace coloured smile as she waved and I gave Anderson a look of disapproval.

"I know you know I secretly wanted to go, see if you were right but at least give me a chance to figure that out because now with what you said we have to go and I don't know to have fun or look for something there," I explained my concern to him as he removed Aliya from me to change her diaper and give me a chance to change my clothes as well as undergarments since he didn't want to see me cold or damp.

"I know you just as well as I know myself. That might sound soon but I know why you wouldn't be able to kill me like you killed Chance even if I really hurt you. I get it because you try to convince yourself that when you're the one doing the hurting it hurts less. That might be the case physically but never mentally or emotionally. You killed once and unless you're inhumane, you wouldn't be able to do it a second time because you'll always feel that pain even when the person you put the physical pain upon is long gone. That's why sometimes I might cross lines and make decisions for you since I know you'd come to that realization too," Anderson truly put things into perspective regarding how much he seemed to know and care about me.

"That might be part of the reason but not the full one because you don't know everything about me," I winked in my attempt to be cute but it allowed him to notice something I didn't desire him to notice.

"Where's your splattered heart marking by your lips? Your hair is still damp, so your face must've hit the water too," he questioned me, allowing my heart to beat a million beats a second as I felt as petrified as I did when I saw the blood on my body, the wounds on my skin that quickly vanished when my mind and body were altered.

"That one thing you might not know is that I couldn't kill someone who made me feel so understood, so loved and in love. I jumped off a cliff-like thing to feel a little carefree after seeing Maddy and didn't feel the pain of the marking tearing into my skin for some reason. I think it's because of you," I lied through my teeth, something I unfortunately became quickly accustomed to.

I knew how Anderson made me feel but was at no place to confidently say I was in love with him. I didn't even know what love was. All I knew was that his body felt good on mine, his eyes understood my own and I remembered who I was more around him when I wasn't caught in a lie. Someone naïve would say that I didn't lie when I said I was in love with him but that I shouldn't have said it so soon.

I say naïve because if you think a girl who accidentally killed anyone close to her if she wasn't already used by them doesn't think she's a monster, then you're wrong. It's tough for her to love her new features, new hair colour without seeing the word evil or bad or sane like the news reporters and even the students at Carry's party that made it too difficult for her to stay. Her knowing what love is is definitely a far stretch.

She associates love with pain because that's all it ever brought her. Love to her will always feel like loss, even the ending to this story supports that. There are days then and now where she'd feel so broken, so torn, so shattered, so unsure as to if worse monsters than her were meant to be happy and she was destined to be all by herself. Some days she doesn't even see herself as company because most days her soul refuses to be there for her. She would spend the days in a dark, lonely room where only the thoughts of others echoed in her mind that were much more terrifying than her own.

Yet every so often he'll come into her mind, remind her that there was a point to her existence, that she was meant to live her own life without being labelled as evil. Just flip the word for yourself.

Another Marble

"Says the party's at seven and unless you know where Olie is, we have to wait until the party to get to know Carry a bit better. Until then, I was wondering if you wanted to do some attempt of an actual date with the baby," I covered up the awkward silence as quick as I could when I lied about my feelings and his pupils grew wide in surprise.

"I have a little idea for this date but we'll be leaving the boat and I know you ended things with Chance today literally and figuratively and that your feelings are probably all over the place and that you shouldn't have said what you did but I feel the same way. Once this baby assessment is over, maybe we can get on with our life away from Matt," he hinted in only a day of knowing me, first as the enemy, then as so much more than that.

"We don't even have jobs, finished our courses? Where did you want to go?" I asked him in utter surprise.

"Anywhere you and I can start a life together is perfect by me. Courses don't matter, school doesn't matter. I'm sure we can find a secluded island where we can gather our food, make a shelter and find warmth. I can still build and imagine us starting our own city where no people are, you can create and establish the entire justice system," he filled my head with the best idea I ever heard.

The idea of living in a world I could create and identify what was wrong and right made me feel in power for the first time in my life. It truly convinced me that running away from your problems, leaving them unfinished and straight for the solution was the way to go.

"You're telling me I can erase my life here and create a new one with you and you're also fine leaving everything behind here?" I clarified, still in surprise that this was even an option. "I can finally start over and choose how everyone sees me," I added in delight.

"Yeah, that's the whole point because you deserve that and so do I. The whole school sees me as some lame nerd whose girlfriend stole all his hard-earned cash. What if I want to be the guy that keeps the girl and lives happily with her for a change? We can do that there, just have to find that place that might not look exactly like the blueprint we made because it would be bigger because we'd start our own world where what others see you as doesn't define you, somewhere we can make our own titles in society and even in the workforce," Anderson suggested as my lips delicately touched his own, just enough to feel a spark I never fully understood but didn't question. "I wish we could leave today but I want to give this baby a good home, a good start and not finishing this project would prevent that..."

"I don't think this baby is meant to be ours. Don't you see how good Maddy is with her? She can tolerate us but I honestly think she needs someone like him or maybe not two teenagers still trying to discover and understand themselves and throwing her into the mix. We'll have a baby when we're ready and we'll look after her for one night and maybe leave her with Maddy since she'll be in capable hands and we'll be gone in the morning while tonight I'll be finding out who we need to make sure doesn't follow us," I suggested and he nodded.

"Your plan sounds better. I'll finalize the details of where we're going and we'll sneak out when Matt's fast asleep," he intrigued me. I couldn't help but grin at the thought of that alone.

That entire day will always be one of my favourites despite the end result because for once in my life I didn't feel like the girl who destroyed everything she touched. I didn't feel like the average person either, felt like the main character in a teen fiction movie, not the side character who was there for support of the main character and everyone else while she gets walked all over and misjudged and that being the end of her story.

We may have done things in the wrong order, may have gone too quick but he did still take me on an actual date. It was my first real date since Chance may have been my first boyfriend but we never labelled spending time together since that's all we could do to make the days fly by, being trapped in a palace and all.

I could spend my entire life recalling every part of that day, some parts of it from a different perspective in any retell or recounting smaller parts that slipped my mind but were just as important. But when I think of that date, I read this notebook entry I wrote that makes it all come back to me.

Shattered were my frustrations, doubts and worries when I was with him. I didn't want a family yet with him because I knew deep down I'd find a way to demolish that too and I did. I stepped out of the house to get some things to pamper myself for our date according to him but in reality, I found Maddy right where I left him and it was as if he knew why I was there, for he handed me a box with a single pill to avoid that potential pregnancy that could've been what I needed for him to stay in my life.

If only I didn't take the pill, things may not have been completely honest but he would've grown to love me, so how bad would that have been? I would've always had someone to care for me, to turn to, because he'd be the family I created all on my own. But that wasn't the solution because if he wanted the same thing as me, he would've found a way even if it was against his morals.

Love goes two ways and has a lot to do with timing, that's about as much as I can say I understand about it. Anderson may have taken me out on a picnic and packed the nastiest attempt at making pasta that I ever had but he made it himself and tried, that's what mattered. He was used to eating the way he had since after taking off from home, living on the streets and slowly starting a life all by himself. He was thankful to be alive and happy for a tough but positive change in his life. He apologized for his cooking and that we could eat out if I preferred but I was more than satisfied with my overcooked, soggy spaghetti in tomato sauce that had charcoal floating in it and was over sweetened.

For three years of my life, I ate palace food that I never had any complaints about despite me wishing that it wouldn't be as complex, yet that food didn't compare to the disaster of a dish in front of me. I ate it with a smile on my face and he pretended to be nervous to put his arm around me when the food was finished and he made his way closer to me, pushing the dishes aside. He tried to be as much of a gentleman as he could despite us sleeping together before the date and us basically feeling like parents with Aliya on our date with us. After all, several people did pass by us in the park to compliment us for adopting a child at such a young age.

We didn't bother explaining to them that it was for a project and I think that's what made me feel so lost in a fantasy world that date. We forgot our containers, blanket and everything there because none of that mattered, just us swinging side by side on the swings with Aliya securely on Anderson's lap. It was weird to live a teenage life I never got to yet also feel so adult-like.

I didn't know simple things about him. I didn't know his favourite colour or favourite animal but I knew about his terrible home life and how to please him in the bedroom. I could easily tell when something was bothering him even when he'd deny it and I had a way of remembering certain phrases that made me laugh or were just adorable.

"I remember swinging so high up once that the bar almost twisted and I thought I had a better chance of jumping off before that happened, broke my leg but it was worth it for the story."

"You are the first girl I've been with since the whole girlfriend stealing my money chaos and I'm glad we were brought together because I haven't genuinely said I've enjoyed myself like this in a long while."

"I'm sorry, I just keep ranting and have a tendency to talk too much about myself. I was that kid everyone would tell in

high school or elementary school to shut up because they heard enough and I want to get to know you too."

These were just a few of the things that stick with me from that day as I instantly saw past the nerd everyone assumed he was with the game he was a part of and the fact that he was good at sketching. He was someone to believe things have a way of working out as they were intended to as am I. He was reckless to a certain extent and one to be honest because he was deceived so much by his girlfriend, Lydia, he trusted dearly. Not to mention, he was aware of his flaws that weren't so much flaws in my opinion as I loved hearing him talk and was fine not talking as much as him since I tended to do the same thing as him and knew I'd do more of the talking the next time.

Sadly, there wasn't a next time and our time went by faster than any well-known sprinter. Darkness slowly began to fill the sky and when Anderson checked his phone to notice that we were already two hours late to Carry's party and had a fussy baby on our hands, we called it an early night.

That's another part of that day I desired to alter because having a friend like Carry in my corner and not being glued to Anderson the entire night at the party would've been better for me. All this day brings me back to is would'ves. Unfortunately, one can't go back to undo what was once done and experiences that hurt never leave us as long as we have a heart.

Even a hardened heart like my own full of pain and tolerance to it constantly aches. Eventually, I'll decide on my own when the aching is enough, when I have suffered enough because like I'll never physically lose myself no matter what happens, I'll never lose the parts of me that make waiting for the day I choose to end all the pain, misery, sorrow I have brought upon myself.

I could've ended it all a long time ago but I saw a point in living, in creating my own family, my own connections, my own story. It isn't over yet even though the original idea shattered and shattered again and again. I still believe the pieces can still fit together in a way I imagined yet couldn't fully predict or comprehend just yet.

I have a habit of reading that entry in my notebook I started writing because of him, when I think back to that day and don't want my thoughts to wonder to the what ifs.

What happened happened and I can't change that. I can't change setting the baby up next to me in Maddy's water bed after I put on a skin tight, beige tank top and chalk grey, drawstring shorts.

I stripped her to her diaper as she seemed a little fussy and overheated from the park although we ensured she was both hydrated and fed there. We didn't have a proper crib for her and I thought her sleeping with us was the best solution so she could easily be monitored and not sleep in a drawer with a cushion.

I began to rock her to sleep in Maddy's bed since the way it jiggled soothed her as I predicted it would. It took much singing softly and talking her through everything before she actually fell asleep. As this was occurring, Anderson prepared all we needed for our escape and joined me in bed not too long later except there was one factor we didn't include in our plan that I only knew the vague details of, and I'm glad we didn't think of it because that factor did more for me than I ever imagined let alone expected.

It was only 9:00 p.m., so I wasn't really tired, just snuggled with Aliya who soon fell fast asleep and I listened to her peaceful coos as I felt as if I was lying in a pool of waves, wondering if a life like this could be real for someone like me. Anderson made me want to believe that but what appears too good to be true usually is. Even those in life who are most fulfilled might feel like they're living a fantasy some days but there will still be parts of those days that the fantasy can be seen through.

I tried not to think about that and promised myself I wouldn't tell Anderson about the pill I took because if we were meant to be parents so young, meant to be a family, redefine the too good to be true saying, the pill wouldn't have worked. Instead, I focused on the little girl I was lucky enough to have in my life for one day and soon felt the warm embrace of Anderson's toned arms around me as we waited to hear Maddy come back on the boat and ditch the baby which we'd leave for him to take care of and then take off completely.

Yet as soon as Anderson interlaced his legs in mine and leaned against me, Maddy entered his room with no duffle bag from before, but was only in his boxers and was soaked from head to toe. He was dripping water from his hair onto the wood floor and left damp footprints on the floor until he approached the bed.

"What happened to you?" Anderson took the words right out of my mouth as he caught Maddy's scraped knee before I did.

"I'm not in the mood to talk about it. But I'm not sleeping in the other bed, gives me old, creepy, haunted house vibes. So unless you guys want to go in that room, we'll take turns with Aliya in here," he suggested.

My eyes met Anderson's in an instant as they grew wide, but he faintly smiled to tell me it would be okay.

That relieved me until Maddy removed his boxers quickly to put on a pair that weren't wet and put the most annoying pair of shorts on top of them. I didn't watch Maddy strip down. I've seen him do it before and never was tempted to look, only looked into his sea-like orbs as I'd have a deep yet casual conversation with him.

"Are you sure you don't want to talk about what happened or at least cover your wound?" I asked him in concern.

"I'll tell you in time, it's just too fresh right now and my knee needs to breathe before it's bandaged. I'll cover it in the morning, Viola, thanks for the concern," he replied kindly, his eyes looking full of waves, fogged up in that sense, full of obstacles he had to overcome to share the burden with someone else to get over. He continued by squeezing his wet hair into the sink of the small bathroom in his room with just a sink and a toilet, and then joined us in bed after drying himself off and wearing beige coloured shorts that reminded me of a man living in a jungle since there were mesh strands hanging from them, mesh strands that felt like sandpaper.

The only thing that got me through that night was the whispers between Anderson and I because I was situated between both men on the bed and the itchy strands on Maddy's shorts were constantly going up and down my legs or just pressing against them as he fidgeted far too often as he slept, constantly tossing back and forth. Maddy even grabbed strands of my hair at one point, mumbling, "Bitch used a sea witch," whatever that meant.

I lied there facing Anderson, us continuously smiling at each other even when Maddy joined us in bed and kept pulling the sand coloured sheets and navy blue and black checkered blanket from us, hogging it all.

"You're all the warmth I need, Lola," Anderson said in a husky voice that allowed me to let go of some of my annoyance from Maddy and secretly wanting Aliya to wake up so I could change where I was situated in the bed.

"I'm always warm, didn't have a lot growing up and got used to not having heat and then when I was in the palace, the silk sheets and everything became too much. I would sometimes even remove the sheet on the mattress and sleep on the bare mattress or the floor with some pillows and a sheet or thin blanket, so he can have all the blankets as long as I can have you, Tommy," I smiled as I softly said each and every word from the heart.

"You were super poor, then filthy rich. When we take off tonight and don't look back, what is it you want to be?" he asked me a more serious question that didn't involve any smiles or casual flirting.

"Even though we'd create our own place where labels such as rich and poor, bad or used don't define us, I'd want to have enough to live comfortably ideally, to avoid that physical struggle. But if we can at least get past that mental struggle, the every day thoughts that make me feel like I'm in a cage I can't get out of or even know where the key is, then the physical struggle will be like a walk in the park. I just want to leave the cage that's always followed me even when I'm out since I'll always feel like different chains or bars are still attached to me and make it feel heavy when I walk...," I opened up to Anderson but stopped as I knew by his reaction and by the fact that Maddy hadn't moved for at least a few minutes, that it was go time.

Anderson slowly got out of bed to see if Maddy would move and when he didn't, he slowly removed Aliya from my arms, not disturbing her as he placed her in Maddy's before she could even fully open her eyes or let out any sounds. Maddy may have been asleep but must've thought I needed a break from her when he opened his closed arms so naturally.

I cautiously followed Anderson's lead as I crept out of bed, trying not to make a single sound as my toes silently grazed the wooden floor, making a slight squeak on occasion but not enough to wake up Aliya or alarm Maddy.

It was when we grabbed our shoes by the edge of the entrance and left the boat without any luggage that I realized something was wrong.

"Did you put bags together already or what exactly are we doing with nothing in our hands?" I questioned Anderson who was also wearing his nightwear, Maddy's teal tank top that hugged Anderson's toned figure and his black sweats with ruby red stripes along the sides.

He didn't say anything just yet, increasing my nerves as he made his way behind me and handcuffed me as a group of police officers exited a black car by the sidelines with weapons by their side as if they thought I would endanger them or try something stupid and childish.

I didn't believe the individuals in navy in front of me, thought it was all a joke or that Anderson hired all of these strippers for entertainment. I didn't know what to ask, what to say, was awaiting him to do the talking and he did. All he said in those few minutes felt like hours, eternity because all crashed around me, shattered like the mirror that morning. The shards of glass that vanished felt as if they didn't disappear as every internal part of me felt pricked.

"I could've done this this morning, had all the evidence to do so, but do like you, Viola. I know you don't love me and were just trying to get me to stay in your life unlike everyone else. I wasn't working for the king but am an undercover cop, the mole at school and that's all you need to know. Everything else can be discussed in court and is my business, nobody else's. If you'd let me, I'd like to get to know you better, maybe continue things since you are an interesting person. But unless you're going to get the punishment you deserve for your actions, I can't be a part of your life. Labels or not, our actions make us who we are; you'll always be courageous in my eyes but you'll also always be a cold-hearted killer until you can redeem yourself," his frigid words still numb my ears to this day as he removed his brown contacts he pretended were as real as his grey eyes, to get me to feel closer to him.

"I'm so much more than that and I know a part of you deep down knows you can see that! I'm not just a criminal. I'm also just a girl standing in front of you, a guy, telling her she really likes him, doesn't understand love but from the parts she gets, she is hopelessly in love after one day because I experienced what so many only get to experience in a lifetime. I'm capable of being loved and loving you, so why does an impulsive action get in the way of that?" I shouted, bloody tears staining my cheeks as I was completely vulnerable in front of him.

"I caught a slight glimpse of that girl and that's why I didn't turn you in this morning. We can be happy, very happy, but not like this, not running away together and I had to do it like this because it was the only way I could put myself through with possibly losing you, just enjoying one moment, one day before that in case you hate me. You just need to trust me, Lola," he muttered between heavy breaths that tickled my neck as he was still behind me, holding me in cuffs.

"Where has trust ever gotten me with you, Tommy? I could get the fucking death penalty and you'd be satisfied because it's the ethical thing! Do you hear yourself?" I yelled at the top of my lungs, my bloodshot tears continued to tumble down my cheeks, staining my neck and tank top.

"I hear myself and I'm saying that I know you made a mistake and like you despite that, just want everyone else to see you like that too and a punishment will make that possible. As hard as it is to not act like kids, there is no place that hasn't already been discovered, no place to start fresh but you can work on yourself as a person to do that. So, I'm not walking away from you because I will always want you and those heart to hearts we had, smiles and laughs shared and I know how determined you are when it comes to justice and I want you to be the best example of that to the world, that's better than any lawyer in my opinion..."

"You're pathetic. I wish you loved me so I didn't have to stop loving you!" I interrupted him, not believing a word that left his lips.

"I tried, I really did. But there comes a point when your hand becomes too heavy to hold without us being separated for a little while first," were his final words to me that I took to heart as he launched me towards the other police officers. "I'll be back for Matt once I have tangible evidence on him but for now, they'll provide you with a lawyer and I'll see you in court," he added as I watched him walk away, taking in the sound of his footsteps against the cement as he headed into another dark vehicle and drove off.

From this experience, I learned that there is a huge difference between not being able to live without someone and loving them. You can have a strong like for so many people in so many different ways, but to feel as if life wouldn't be the same or be able to go on without them, that was something I had yet to experience.

I was afraid that what I had with Anderson couldn't be found again. I may have told a lie or two that would've bite me where it hurts if things did work out but it was obvious he lied to me about who he was as an individual and his life. He wasn't a protector or a lover which I assumed correctly. But he wasn't the man I thought he was, someone who could understand me and feel my presence when I wasn't there like I constantly felt his for a little while. Instead, he was a marble on the cement ground.

He wasn't an ordinary pebble or something you wouldn't pick up because it was boring. He stood out because it was as if our paths were meant to cross since someone else hadn't taken the place I wanted to in his life. Yet just because a marble shows interest in those who can't help but find their eyes in its direction, doesn't mean it's important.

A marble is something many young children fascinate over, especially if they aren't used to having the newest gadgets to play with. If someone like myself constantly feels misjudged, trapped or in a corner observing the lives that all made my own look like it was underdeveloped, a marble will appeal to them as if its gold. In reality, it is better than being trapped with those who don't want to be there with you, those that backstab you in ways they don't view as manipulation because they are so accustomed to doing that or just oblivious to it all. But it is just a stepping stone to what you do deserve.

Simplicity and feeling heard are great things but what about feeling cared for and looked after during the moments you feel most by yourself? What about finding someone who remembers all the details you have to say, even those you forget? The person who will do whatever it takes to talk to you even if things are broken, awkward or the timing isn't great. This is a paperclip. It was dropped on the concrete, the ground level you constantly walk on and feel as if you can never get ahead of. It isn't simple and beautiful like the marble but it blends in with the concrete, might blend into your background, life, as if it always belonged, just awaiting you to notice it, notice him. That is when you know that the marble wasn't the one that got away but your introduction to real feeling that isn't all sunshine and rainbows, real feeling you can see and experience up close for a change.

It might come back to you as marbles constantly roll but it doesn't mean it's right for you. The pain associated with it will ease with time and you'll even be able to be civil with the marble but you wouldn't go back there if given the chance because if the marble was anything like the paperclip, it wouldn't roll for even a second. It would be happy to even be sharing the concrete with you and enjoying the moments you have or exploring your separate similar yet different lives that have a way of meeting eventually. If it was anything like the paperclip, it would've waited for its time, not jumped into something it knew it couldn't stay in just yet.

When thinking back to Anderson, I don't regret a thing because I now understand that he wasn't important, just a tool to lead me towards the shed where everything I've ever desired lies. That was where I noticed the paperclip wedged into my shoelace for the first time officially.

Soulless

Being convicted as a prisoner felt a lot like when I was told to head to the principal's office, except I wasn't spoken to, only stripped down. The only difference this time was that I wasn't alone.

I was escorted from a cop car that didn't have to drive too far with the prison only being a bridge away, to a dreary grey building with sand coloured floors where my handcuffs were undone and I was patted down before the cop turned around and gave me a chance to put on the baggy orange jumpsuit. It was then that I realized I wasn't alone as I witnessed marks all over my legs that looked like stamps.

"You're underage," one said. "You're mentally unstable," another read. "Goodbye," the last of the dark smudges that dug into my skin added.

It was made obvious why Maddy scratched my legs so much that night. He found out the truth but saved me in the only way he saw fit because he knew that that summer school, that town was no place for a criminal and that Anderson would put him behind bars if not for killing his parents, then for killing whoever he did that night. There was another word I almost didn't notice because it wasn't stamped, but written in red pen as if it was the most important thing. "Survival" the slanted handwriting stated.

That single word alone brought me back to a moment with Maddy. I was told countless times that to survive, I either needed to be myself or anything but myself. And anytime I committed actions that were against my morals, I blamed survival as the factor for that.

When I first met Maddy and felt that instant closeness when I laid on his almost bare body as I wore his blouse, he told me something I don't associate with that warmth I felt.

"Survival sometimes means killing like animals but we do it for a better tomorrow even if our insides feel numb or fucked up," I remember him understanding my entire life better than me before he even knew anything about me.

I didn't feel warm or comforted by his words and body in that moment which is why I associate it as separate from a moment that made me feel all that.

Those words will always be stuck in my head as a reminder that we may be born alone and die alone but that doesn't mean we are alone. There will always be someone that understands us, thinks like us and if we're lucky enough to even catch a glimpse of them, then we understood life through eyes that weren't our own but felt like them. Life to me will always feel like one big mystery that the only thing I can fully say I know about it is that if all you do is survive, you haven't lived just yet.

The red words on the side of my leg reminded me that a part of Maddy felt like it would never fully belong to him just like with myself because we never fully had the chance to explore what it was we desired to get out of the world. The day I started to know him was the day he began to follow my lead and not constantly protect himself, not constantly survive. So why leave me with that horrific word? Why go back?

When one thinks that in order to get the chance to live, one must survive, it's easy to go back to that instinct. It's easy to kill again despite the guilt associated with it.

I had no solid evidence but knew he killed again and that's why he wrote out his plan to save me instead of telling me. He was forced to run, go far, far away, yet he felt so close.

He felt so close because he'd always be a protector. He always found ways to look out for me without coming off as clingy, in my way or even when we'd disagree. He came up with a plan to save me from jail time and possibly being executed.

It was only in a few words, all he managed to leave me to save us both yet I understood it instantly as if our minds were one. It occurred to me with his words that I was only 17 until the following day and didn't even know Anderson's real age. It could easily help my case or help him land some time in jail since he had sex with a minor. The insanity bit that I could blame on my childhood could also prevent jail time or a death penalty as it would be replaced with a rehabilitation centre.

It was those few words that helped me in deciding the best way to find justice in a terrible situation. I was going to be everything everyone saw me as. It went against my morals, my beliefs but if I could get myself out of a bad situation by blindsiding all those around me as they have blindsided me, that's the most righteous thing I could do. And I didn't want to be provided with a lawyer who couldn't tell my made-up story as good as I could, so I didn't use the one I was provided. I chose to represent myself, something I was quite accustomed to with how many people wiped their muddy feet all over my carpet of a life.

I put on the orange jumpsuit instantly as I didn't want them to think I was doing anything illegal, especially since my undergarments had gems on them I could use as weapons if needed. I was told I'd be spending the rest of the day and night in jail and that the court hearing would be the following day, on my 18th birthday. I could have thought of so many better ways to spend it than being imprisoned but I did have the chance to be the lawyer I never did become.

Following me being put in my orange uniform, was I escorted towards a cell with one other girl in it who I only saw once but recognized in an instant.

"Technically, we can't put you behind bars for good until tomorrow's trial. So, you'll be here temporarily with this woman who may or may not be a prostitute," a tall, slightly heavy police officer with dirty blonde hair explained in a serious tone but I knew better as what he said was far from the truth.

"Thank you, officer. I'll be sure to behave myself until tomorrow's trial I want to represent myself in," I stated firmly as he rolled his eyes.

"Good luck with that, sweetheart," he muttered sarcastically as I pictured popping his large belly with a pin while he unlocked the cell and pushed me in it with the woman with the bedazzled orange jumpsuit.

"You're not a prostitute, so why are you here?" I whispered to her the moment the police officer by the name of Gary left our side after instructing her to tell me the rules for today.

"Matt had a few things you needed to hear. He's gone now and didn't tell me where, just that he hopes you understood his message. He found out Anderson's plan when he was out with Harmony because Anderson wasn't in on it alone and Harmony isn't exactly his sister but his girlfriend who has been trying to get so much out of Matt for years to survive, not only dirt but for someone like him to fall in love with her. There are cameras everywhere, I can't say much more than that but your exact thoughts are right, that's what he said because you two have a habit of sharing thoughts," the girl whose party we were supposed to go to stood in front of me, explaining the brief details of things that lined up in my head minus why she was the one telling me this. Why her out of everyone? How would she know?

"Carry, thank you, but how did you get in here and why are you telling me this? It seems strange that you invited us to your party and have a past with uh Matt and he suddenly seems to trust you now with so much and ask you to do so much when you guys used to hook up and some people think he made you a lesbian," I admitted to her honestly as she sat on the hard, cement ground with her legs crossed and gazed up at me with her caramel coloured eyes.

"I knew you said you were going to come by and when you didn't show, I saw it as weird, just wanted to make sure everything was okay. I approached the boat a little past nine and didn't see you but saw Anderson making out with Harmony as he whispered that all would be over really soon and that Matt didn't even need to marry her to save her, just needed to fall in love with her, what he was too closed off to do. She wore a beyond revealing skin tight dress where the top was connected strings barely covering her titties, saying she had her ways. She took off and I followed her to see her to see stuff I never wanted to but felt the need to help with," she hinted at the worst. I gazed at her in wonder as to how she knew to follow her and not monitor Anderson. "You could handle yourself, Maddy can't and I know that about him. That's why I followed her and it was a good thing I did so you guys can have a proper see you later. I have some notes he wanted to leave you with," she finished her explanation and gestured for me to sit on the dirty metal toilet where no camera was aimed towards. That was where she handed me a crumpled up, large map with writing on the back.

Viola,

Read the following myth that isn't a myth. I stumbled upon it recently because believe it or not, I do read. Mermaids exist in the same waters I laid my boat in. They are soulless creatures who look to be loved by those who originally stole their souls, pirates, and sell their voices to sea witches to temporarily have legs to appeal to humans. If loved by pirates, they appear more human-like and eventually will have a full life as a human if wed. I threw her back into the waters she came from and she tried her hardest to come back up since she lost her mermaid-like features, I cut her where it hurt most and pushed her down. I didn't want to but felt the need to. I'm not proud of what I did but if I didn't destroy her, with time she would've destroyed me. You and I share a lot of similar thoughts, what you're picturing happened is what did. I needed to leave that behind along with my real identity. I'll find ways to see you, to know where you are because someone needs to make sure you're okay.

- Maddy

    I held the tattered, sand coloured paper that reminded me of a pirate map, between the tips of my fingers and vividly could see the gruesome event unfold in front of my very own eyes.

    There stood Maddy by the cliff I thought he was going to end it all. He stood there with a slim smile one would believe was genuine but I knew better than that.

    He stared at Harmony in her revealing dress as if he sensed her arrival. He gazed at her from top to bottom, undressing her with his eyes and devouring her in his mind as he licked his rough, chapped lips.

    "Your brother must've told you I packed a suit and had the prom we missed out on planned for you. That is sort of the truth except for the fact that I want you to wear the suit. I know you have a weird thing for guys in dresses," he hinted and as she removed her dress without thinking twice, did he try to push her off the edge of the rocky area, knowing her sea-like qualities faded for the most part.

"And what exactly do you think you're doing, you wanted criminal?" she barked at him, wearing nothing other than her lacy, maroon coloured panties while she pulled against his force.

"I'm not a criminal and you know that better than anyone," he explained firmly.

"You tempted me and then pushed me, so I don't know what to think…"

"Liar!" he interrupted her, pushing himself closer to her and her closer to the edge as she tried to back away, and random pieces of seaweed jumped up from the water to wrap around her breasts and legs. "That has happened anytime you go near the water, shells, waves, seaweed cover your body like it belongs on it. So tell me what I think I've known for a while but didn't know the why to!" he shouted at her.

"That's why you tried to throw me in the water? We made love in the water this morning. I lost my tail a long time ago if that's what you're referring to…"

"That wasn't love. This isn't love. I thought it was a long time ago and still think about us almost bringing a child into the world and know you tampered with that box to force us to be closer and why that wasn't meant…"

"Don't you dare say we weren't meant to be! When we first met, I had no voice and we communicated through eye contact and our bodies!" she interrupted him, protesting as her arms flung all over the place.

Maddy immediately rolled his eyes. "I didn't care you couldn't speak then because I just wanted you undressed and under me. I only was individually with you when you fell pregnant. I only cared about you when there was something bigger than us both involved!" he exclaimed, breaking her heart as she witnessed so much truth behind them but his cold, numb eyes, felt warm to me, familiar. I knew there was a point he did love her and a part of him that always will despite her manipulating him.

"You're a fucking liar!" she shrieked.

"Must be a better one than you because if you think you're going to live off my soul, you have another thing coming, bitch!" he stated strongly while she didn't cry or look tarnished like a normal person, instead cackled.

"It's either you let yourself fully love me like I know you want to or you rot in jail for the rest of your life until you kill yourself like your mom killed herself. The threat note was my idea to make things more fun and your mom's handwriting is easy to copy, it being in the newspaper and all since she was a writer and your brother thought a poem she wrote with her own two hands along with the death announcement fit well," her laugh grew louder and then silent as she attempted to maintain a serious tone she believed would get to him.

"I'm not even going to bother reacting to that but do need to know what you have on me besides your word alone that thinks I would even commit a crime," Maddy played the clueless part perfectly while shrugging his shoulders to fully sell it.

"Well, for one, there's the picture of you and Viola that would paint you as her accomplice in court. And as for your past, your new identity has many flaws in the office paperwork that I snooped through as per Anderson's request…"

"Why do that for him?" he questioned her, interrupting her as per usual.

"Because he gave me my legs for a request of going for a pirate that did him well. I lost my voice first as a test to see if you really loved me. He wanted my voice to use to lure other criminals since it's such a gentle voice but said I could keep it, if I could get his number one target, why he became a cop and posed as a student at the summer school, to fall for me and tell me everything. And something they don't tell you about mermaids is that they may be soulless but they have the best memory which is a curse since we are promised a gruesome afterlife in the sea foam where that acts as our only entertainment while you get an afterlife full of light, embrace, happiness and goodness. That memory remembers all the little pieces you told me about your past here and there and knows the big picture and when I die, it will be revealed. Mermaids with souls have long lives, but I'm not that with what you said, so your secret will be known to the world soon enough. Those you care about dearly will figure it out when they come across your handwriting or anything personal really of you and the word will slowly spread, not through that object but through the universe as if it was always a known fact," Harmony explained to him honestly while Maddy grabbed something out of the suit pocket he hid and what I first assumed were drawstring shorts but realized in that moment was a grey scarf he fetched and put around her neck. He confused her as he wrapped it tightly, choking her as she swung her arms at him as they both tumbled off the cliff, landing awkwardly in the water as they made loud splashes.

I couldn't see either one in the aqua blue water until Maddy popped his head out of the water, breathing heavily as he swam after the girl who lost her tail but was still a strong swimmer. "I had a feeling you have been using me for a while, did my own fucking research on your kind and it didn't help when I see you looking at Anderson when I went to grab my fishing rod and then headed back to the stream in a hurry to beat you there. You looked at him the way Viola deserved to be looked at by him. But karma's a bitch since it's obvious he is just using you but it's obvious you tried to like me all these years because you wanted him to love you," he voiced to her in a low voice that did the trick with the depth behind it and allowed her to make her way closer to him. It was that second where he fetched a small blade he hid in his suit and carved a heart into her neck, around the area her voice box would be. Little streak by little, did she grow weaker and weaker as she didn't bother fighting, only screamed until her screams could no longer be heard as the waves blocked them out.

However, a few words did stand out prior to her entire body going pale and then lifeless. "Thank you," she muttered her final words during her final breath.

A girl without a soul is a girl with no afterlife that made the pain worth it. When one dies, their body stays on earth and their soul goes up above or down below, the fate they deserve. Without a soul and only a body, there isn't anything to you that meets your outer appearance. There's no inner beauty, no purpose to keep you going when life has you down, no reason for your body to exist in this world. So, hers didn't. With a sharp yet small blade to the throat, she disappeared but didn't leave without a trace. She left Maddy a few sparkles in the water to represent the shallow creature she was expected to be. However, soul or not, she did have a mind of her own and did understand feeling to some extent even though it wasn't right for her.

Maddy left for both of our sakes with what I found out through his handwriting and what the rest of the world would soon enough know. That didn't make it easy for him to run with no place to hide and an undetermined amount of time until everyone knows who he is. Yet he killed her then because he was done being hurt by her, didn't want to see her oblivious to how much she deserved, wanted her to see and understand it all, even from the sea foam that has a way of resurfacing in the water. She knew that, that's why she thanked him and she knew that her and I were quite alike when it comes to loving someone that will never love us the same or feeling as if the entire world is against you, as if your fate was supposed to be cursed.

Due to this similarity, she didn't fight him, had let go, because Maddy didn't address how she looked at him, but how she looked at another man that betrayed me. He carved a heart into the part of her that came later that he fell for but didn't fall for him like that, the part she didn't use to lie for once but to be grateful to watch the rest of the story unfold from two perspectives. Two perspectives that shared similarities with each other and with her. She shattered parts of both worlds by making their lives harder that felt like they were just falling into place for the first time in a long time. Yet ironically, she was the one who could watch us when we couldn't watch each other; watch the world unfold when both Maddy and I were trapped from it, just not together.

That paper that told me so much and made me feel like I was there was what I used as toilet paper that night since we didn't have any. I was done sulking because that didn't change anything, wouldn't have altered where I am now.

I did what I knew how to do most, what Maddy knew how to do most, better than me. He didn't only kill her for rage but for righteousness like with his dad. I didn't think about how Chance's death would affect Sophia or if he had any family that cared about him. That was all that was on my mind the next day however. Yet that night, survival began to mean more than just selfishness.

The Villain in His Story

Survival that night meant trying to sleep after doing jail chores and thanking Carry for the letter and for being there. It meant putting my strategies to a close so I'd be well rested enough to make sense the following day.

I did constantly squirm in my attempt to get comfortable on the cold, cement floor until I managed to get tuckered out as my eyes did close and I did have a plan for the following day in mind. It was a darn good plan but I didn't follow it. That's what happens when you're actually in the moment you picture in your mind; there's a huge difference.

In my head, I stood up there strong as I stated all Maddy had wrote on my body. I stated my story, my feelings that consumed me that made me psychotic. Yet I knew that was anything but true. However, I found out that in court, I wasn't telling a signal lie.

I stood in place, so strong in an orange jumpsuit, pleading my case all alone, how my entire life felt and that's what made me sound so crazy, crazy enough to be locked up, just not in jail.

A judge in a powdered wig, how typical. A police officer I will never feel myself in front of because he blindsided me more than anyone I ever met, stood by the opposing side with a proper lawyer as he fought for the man I killed who was his brother, that's why he cared so much. Apparently he was Maddy's too, a fact his mother never told them since Anderson and Chance were her past mistakes with a different man that wasn't Maddy and Olie's father.

Anderson may have lied about the details of his past but not about the feelings associated with it. His mom abandoned him when things became too difficult with his trapped brother, so he took off, running away from his dad who became reliant on alcohol and was looking for a fresh start. Being a police officer was an obvious choice since he was tired of things being unjust in his own life and desired to find the man who he saw as responsible for killing his mom he never stopped loving despite her starting a new life with a new man and having children with him at a much older age.

I was asked about Maddy's whereabouts when I was brought up to the stand but honestly had no idea, just as Maddy intended. The case was shortly turned to me, the girl who killed his only brother, his last sane family member that cared for him, but the background of it all allowed me to understand the eyes that weren't brown like my own but were just as dark, just as gloomy.

I was the villain in his story and everyone else's. I felt as much pain by his betrayal that he likely did through his brother's death, who Thomas flipped his last name so I wouldn't put two and two together.

In his defense, he was getting even. Yet he only knew the surface of what I underwent growing up. He didn't understand how lucky I felt growing up with my new guardians who loved and cared for me yet how unlucky and poor I appeared in the eyes of others. It always seemed to be the eyes of others that dictated how I felt or how I was supposed to feel anyways and if I didn't feel like that, they found a way to make me feel like that.

My entire life I was constantly molded into worlds I had no desire to be a part in. I always felt like a goldfish, trapped in a tank too small and predictable for those outside but massive to her. Why feel bad for a fish without knowing her story? Why assume that space is so little?

Societal norms are easier to agree with. Standing out makes it harder to live. But when one continues to fall after hurt, pain, betrayal, three things that follow her in her small tank full of enriching experiences yet however make her crave to jump out of the tank, feel more than this. What more do you need when you're accustomed to it and familiar with the outcome? The feeling is almost numbing, if only the end result could feel different if the experiences associated with these emotions also brought love to make up for it.

In an orange jumpsuit, in front of no faces that felt familiar, not even Anderson's as he felt like a stranger, a man who was good with words and blinded me with them, words that hid his dreadful actions, did I feel like that fish I had to pretend I wasn't okay being. That tank was good for me, I just had to wait for those repetitive feelings to alter as the monotony of them would teach me a valuable lesson that makes the tank feel massive, full of possibility.

"I was never given a fair chance. I was never in control in my own life, given choices that were mine. Every choice I made was made for me by others or I was manipulated to think they were my own! So, I stand here, representing myself because I am the only one who can do an accurate representation of me because unlike everyone who thinks they know who I am, I don't know what I am because I always let others define me. I know killing wasn't what I had in mind for Chance but I also didn't think my first love would betray me, a man I knew I was supposed to love in my story but noticed that we weren't as similar as I thought. I'm much more similar to his brother, Thomas, willing to use one's insecurities to push them down like how I've been treated my entire life, just to not feel like I'm in this alone. But I know what I did to survive made another family weak and when we lose those close to us, we're never alone because we all experienced loss in some shape or form. Survival is done best in packs, not alone and for that, I shouldn't have let my emotions make my pack grow. I should have..."

"We heard enough, Ms. Marley. Mr. Nosredna's lawyer has not even stated his facts yet and the jury has already spoken," the judge cut me off like everyone else had a habit of doing, judging me before they knew me.

"How is that even fair? Did he tell you that he had sex with me yesterday when I was still a minor? Did he tell you that he pretended to understand me, to know me? Did he tell you that he pretended to be the same age as me? I wouldn't have gotten involved with him if I knew he was much older! He toyed with my emotions, my body, my heart! And just because I killed a man, that makes me guilty? I ended the life of a man who almost did as much damage as his brother with the fantasy he created, a life I could choose, yet he treated me as he did to get to princess Sophia, so it wasn't really my choice after all. Does that make me guilty? At least I was strong enough to end his misery then and there and not put an emotional toll on him that would've lasted forever!" I screamed until my throat felt as raw as my emotions and as bloody as the tears that stained my cheeks.

"Mrs. Genevie, how old is your client?" the judge asked the lawyer with the black, stringy hair yet stern expression, unfazed by his question.

"My client is 23 but the intercourse was consensual and Ms. Marley was 17 when it took place. She may be considered a minor, however, the age of legal consent is 16 and he is not an authoritative figure, was not a teacher that forced himself upon her, your honour," she stated in her monotone voice while Anderson sat there, not saying a single word as he held his head in his crossed arms as he just desired for things to be over. It was obvious things were painful for him although his gelled back hair and fancy suit said he was put together. He could've been playing the part well of the victim or things could've felt more real and he truly was grieving his brother.

"Jury, you are dismissed. The accused does not need any verdict to tell her if she is guilty or not. She knows that and she will be enrolled into an institution of wellness, a psychiatric hospital. She will receive the required treatment and live in that healthy environment for the remainder of her life. Her prison sentence would have been a life time sentence, not the death penalty but it will be spent in this hospital. As for the defendant, he will take a month's time away from the force because he is grieving and cannot let that get in the way of his work again. He will be required to receive therapy during that time..."

"Do I look like I'm fucking someone who needs therapy?" Anderson stood up to irrationally make a point that irritated me.

"At least you don't have to live a life where you've never made a single choice that was truly yours and now know that will never change! I'd rather have received the death penalty, have ended it all once and for all!" I exclaimed in utter fury, fire erupting in my body and making its presence known that the judge ushered for a few jurors to hold me back as I stood on top of the desk I was behind to make my presence known.

I was pulled off the desk and carried into a white pickup truck that took me to the mental institution that would be my new palace but don't remember how I got there. Suddenly, a sharp needle held by a tall, older man in a white lab coat entered my body. The last thing I remember from the court date was turning back to my left to not focus on the man in the lab coat but Anderson who I studied his grey eyes as if he did feel something for me and was attempting to distance himself after the cruel rejection that he deserved.

The needle that was inserted in my skin as if I was an animal and the sleep and drowsiness associated with it made me feel as if I had hibernated for a long winter. The needle knocked me out for a full day. My entire 18th birthday was a blur that began with waking up in a cell without a cellmate as she was only in to give me the note and was released shortly after. My birthday ended with me being molded into someone I wasn't for the rest of my life, to only then waking up in a single bed in a white hospital gown.

My limbs ached a burning sensation as they were on the bed for far too long. Yet I couldn't even change my position as my arms and legs were chained to the bed as if I was going to kill myself since I was the only person in the clean, fully white room, walls and floor. No furniture laid in the room other than the all white bed I was in, wooden frame and all. There however was one item that stood out in the room full of monotony, a poorly drawn teddy bear drawn on the wall in black marker.

"You never had the chance to be a kid," I could hear his exact words. "You deserve to not have Gloria know where you are because you deserve to feel free, in control, reckless, like consequences don't exist. You deserved to have a teddy bear."

"A teddy bear? I grew up poor. Why would I want something so useless..."

"It's not useless. It's comforting. It's something you can hug when you're all by yourself and feel helpless. It can't judge you like everyone else. It can't define you, can only listen," he interrupted me to cure my confusion and continued to steer the ship towards summer school, as if he had to say no more and we could just stay there in silence and still know we cared for each other.

It may sound like a farfetched theory, but I knew he drew that bear and did tear up when a care worker entered my room and noticed what it was I was smiling at. She instantly made me frown as she returned with white paint and covered the bear up.

"We want no negativity here, no dark energy, only light. You've been asleep for around a day but you were fed by a machine, so you shouldn't feel too light headed. I am going to remove the cuffs if you remain calm and we can explore your room together," a middle-aged, short woman with a soothing voice and a white button-up, short sleeve dress that matched the room, along with her straight, silver hair that landed a little above her chin, explained to me.

I nodded as my words in the court room got me to this room. I buried my sadness deep down without any tears shed as although the bear wasn't visible as she painted over it, I knew it was on the wall. I knew it was there and knew that Maddy may have been gone from my life yet he'd still always manage to be a part of it.

The Constant Visitor

The caregiver removing my handcuffs didn't make me feel any less trapped. Being in the arms of a good friend and even being in a kiss I didn't expect or desire but found so calming and even freeing when one of my heart markings vanished, was the opposite of being trapped.

I felt like a bird whose wings weren't clipped any longer yet I was still in a cage. I desired the key to exit the cage and roam without limits.

As the days went by in which were spent in monotony as the useless training to be something I wasn't didn't do me well, did I receive several signs from him that all would be alright.

I didn't understand how he did so or even why he cared so much but he managed to always make me smile.

The bear on the wall was the only thing that was drawn and I was positive he drew it. The day Anderson drew me a blueprint of a life that would never work because our philosophies were too different and the betrayal erased any feeling I thought I had for him, was the same day Maddy drew a few items in permanent marker on wooden floorboards.

I vividly remember noticing them after we were assigned the baby project and when Maddy convinced

Anderson and I to conserve water. On the way to the bathroom, I remember in the awkwardness of it all, glancing down at the floor as we approached a moment that was flooded with emotion and intimacy,

It obviously wasn't the main focus but did ease my nerves ever so slightly. Seeing a terribly drawn home in black marker which was literally just a pentagon with a heart drawn in it, told me that home was where the heart is. Shortly after that floor board laid another one with what I assumed was a violet as it was the only picture coloured to show what it was with all of its purple petals plucked as they laid on the ground to form a heart, telling me that inner beauty is what matters most. Lastly, there was one more floor board in which an apple laid with a heart carved into the centre.

All the drawings looked as if a four-year-old could've done a better job with them but were simple enough to make out what they were, just like the bear. I didn't understand the apple one until I thought back to the other drawings the day the teddy bear showed up and then disappeared from the wall. Even then it didn't make sense why someone would love something as ordinary as an apple.

The following day one appeared on my bed with a piece missing, so I could see how black the core was. The day after that, the piece that was missing was on a white plate which read, "Nothing is evil" in ruby red paint. I glanced at the piece of apple itself to notice a slit in the apple slice where I pulled out a folded white slip of paper.

Violence isn't okay, let's avenge.

The scribbly handwriting matched the letter I received in prison and it did sound like something Maddy would say.

Without even putting it into words, it was a well known fact to us both that violence isn't physical. Violence is a build-up of emotions that hit us when we least expect it, punch us where it hurts most yet leaves no physical mark, just invisible bruises we are forced to see and those that truly care about us and want to see those too.

The sentence Maddy wrote had the first letter of each word slightly on an angle to make it obvious he spelled out my name, what makes me myself. It was almost as if he was telling me he knew my invisible bruises too well yet still wanted to find ways to explore them.

He was trying to tell me that violence wasn't who I am, may have given me a dark core to show me that my trauma doesn't define me but how I utilize what I experienced does.

He was trying to show me that darkness can fade away when treated with the right care. It didn't have to be bleach blonde or jet black but could be a caramel brown. Darkness will always exist in me as it does in everyone but I won't let it define me. Slowly my hair did get lighter, same with my eyes and my smile. I'm not referring to in colour but in weight.

My feet that stood heavily on the ground, suddenly didn't feel as if they had to try so hard to do more than stand straight and survive. For once they felt capable of living. My arms that once stood stiff by my side flapped like wings of a bird, so free and capable.

The darkness in my hair and eyes felt lighter although it did appear the same colour. Darkness can't completely vanish because of how tainted it is. Yet what is tainted can be cleaner even though it might not be noticeable. Some of the nicest people have the dirtiest faces. To see past that takes someone with very open or similar eyes.

Reminders that he was still with me, my protector, Madison Chambers, told me that I met that person and will continue to feel him if we can't see one another again.

It was a strange feeling to grow up not seeing him but seeing him through others. I didn't receive any visitors except for Anderson who did beg me to give him another chance, saying something along the lines that, "If you don't give me another chance, you'll never feel loved."

The girl with the light hair and eyes would've broken down into tears, would've maybe even given him another chance but I wasn't her. She was long gone. She was weak, brittle, innocent and good. I'm none of those things. I didn't know what I ever longed for with Anderson because what we experienced was anything but love. He was beyond two-faced as he only showed me what I desired to see yet now looking back on things, I'm not so quite sure what I saw was even what I wanted.

I didn't need a man to build a house with me but a man I could be anywhere and still feel at home, still feel him because he is my home. I had that since I entered the boat just didn't see it or understand it. I lost the splattered heart near my lips because the only person that was ever meant to kiss them did. Not Anderson or Chance or a boy in elementary school that kissed me on a dare or even my own hand when I was practicing what it would be like to kiss Chance who I counted as my first kiss since it went both ways. But it was the man who grew up with what is traditionally a girl's name yet was the man I never saw coming.

I saw this man most through one constant visitor who I didn't have to tell security to keep out. However, that visitor didn't start coming until I was in my mid-20s. This visitor was young, a boy whose mom was one of the nicer nurses I could actually be myself in front of and not have to play so nice and proper with. He would call me a queen and made me paper crowns anytime his mom was in which we'd hide from the other nurses.

Nolan was his name, a sweet, six-year-old boy, whose mom was a saint to raise him all by herself when she didn't even ask for him in her life. He was left on her doorstep with a message to take him to her job since the old queen was his mother, me, and would know exactly what to do with him when he's around the age of the princess she once saw as a daughter.

I was struck by disbelief but the woman who had been looking after him, Morine, didn't even have him call her mom, that's how much of a believer she was in that boy being meant for me. I knew it wasn't possible as I had no recollection of being pregnant and any chance of that with Anderson was removed. There was always the idea of a male nurse raping me but I was never unconscious for more than a day and that was if I talked back to a nurse. It was impossible I wouldn't have known I was having a baby, especially since it would exit the other end of me in a beyond painful process.

It didn't make any sense to me, just like some random guy letting me live with him for as long as I needed without a full explanation right away, on his boat. He didn't know who I was yet knew I was in trouble and wanted to be the person he didn't have when he was in trouble.

That little boy with the honey brown, stringy hair needed me and I wasn't about to question why. I managed to raise him with Morine's assistance as I would spend the days with him and he would spend the nights with her.

Although, I thought I was meant to keep him safe and out of trouble, he was brought there to do that for me and he came bearing so many stories that made it feel as if I wasn't just getting through the days or hoping for better, but actually living them and not desiring for them to come to a close.

It was as if he had a webcam on Maddy because he saw all I missed. He'd mumble things like, "This guy camped out after running away from his troubled home. He only had two pieces of wood he used for fire and slowly found more that became a boat." The boy had a habit of talking really fast and in full sentences of a boy much older than his age, making it obvious that Morine truly did a good job raising him.

He knew stories he wasn't old enough to have seen but old enough to understand when being told them. I had assumed that he knew Maddy or ran into him at some point or another, that was why he was brought to me. But the truth was difficult to pinpoint when the boy would tell me what Maddy was doing at that point in time, almost as if he was psychic.

He didn't tell me where he was, either because he didn't know or didn't desire for me to escape and find him. Nolan never told me the exact reason but his eyes said it all. His eyes said what the waters couldn't.

Although the boy did backtrack me in my progress along with the caregiver who nobody saw but me, I knew Maddy would believe what I saw. I knew he wouldn't think I was crazy and I knew he'd make me truly feel at home again.

What I didn't know was how. How he'd get to me, how we wouldn't both be thrown in jail, how we'd live happily ever after if that was a thing for people like us. Yet none of that mattered.

With the stories I was told, the ways I got to know and feel Maddy without him being there, made me hopeful for a future with him. The empty space I was in that almost felt like a fresh start just not quite since I couldn't be my true self, made me feel as if I had a slight say in my destiny. It wasn't a huge say but it was a start in reading the script in a different way than I had began.

Freedom In A Mirror

I was in a new space I couldn't exactly be my true self in but that new space was what I needed to find myself, understand the other half to me that was missing.

I was in a new palace full of possibility, full of blank space, whiteness, dullness I planned to see colour through and that's what I did.

I'd wake up in the morning with a smile on my face during the days I was trusted without cuffs on which soon became every day. The less I said, the more I felt heard, so I spoke to nobody other than the boy when nobody was near me or did so subtle enough to not raise suspicion.

However, the more I looked forward to seeing Nolan, the less I saw of him. I tried not to think about him so I'd see him more yet that method was proven to be useless. The more I attempted to not think about him, the more he was on my mind and the closer he was to vanishing completely.

He didn't take long to fully disappear but I didn't feel abandoned with all the memories he left me with. He'd run around my room that didn't save space for much more than my bed and would use the sheets as a cape. Nolan would pretend to soar in the sky like a hero. He would do so on my bed on his knees yet would never fall.

He'd slide along my bed, sometimes playfully tumble but was never hurt or sad as if his sole purpose was to accompany me and to fill my mind with stories of what could've been.

I vividly recall sitting along the edge of my bed, awaiting dinner to be served as Nolan tugged the edge of my white gown. "Dance with me," he ordered. "Practice for your wedding," he continued in his soft, innocent voice that wouldn't have said such words if he was much older and understood why I was destined to be alone.

"I know I'm in white but what makes you think someone like me should get married?" I questioned him with a slight laugh as I let his sea-like orbs consume me as I held his small hands and we danced around in circles.

I was pulled into the depths of the water, locking my eyes with the woman who was partly responsible for me being in a mental institution. Features of her that matched Nolan's, such as her narrow nose and full lips flashed as if lightning hit them. She then disappeared entirely into the unknown as the water filled with blood, her blood Maddy was responsible for.

I could see his hands pushing the blood aside as he killed her but wasn't a killer, there's a major difference. He saved her in a way even the strongest wouldn't have the strength to do because they'd see it as unjust. Those same eyes that took away the beauty from the bloodshed sea, looked away from his mess and right at me.

I could feel him in that moment and saw a flash of his entire life as if it were my own. Blood and tears were present in every other memory. I never saw him cry in my life. I saw him wet, bruised, jealous, stuck on words, with blood near him, but never tears.

Yet as a child, tears were all he understood. His parents would argue, his dad would beat his mom until she could barely stand yet would stop when he'd see tears leave her cheeks. He understood those tears as a cry for help and shed those same tears when he used his dad's own hunting gun and shot him to break up a fight between his parents that hadn't yet become physical. He didn't shoot his dad once but twice to ensure he was gone. He desired to shoot him a third time but his mom's loud cries and shrieks stopped him.

He cried the moment he noticed her crying because he thought what he did would end all her tears, would finally make her happy. That was why he ignored her cries for him to stop until it was too late. She put on a fake smile for him but he wondered why he wasn't woken up for school the following day and his brother woke him up instead. Maddy ran into his mom's room as a result of this with his brother who was frozen and could barely speak after what he just laid eyes on.

There they witnessed their mom's lifeless body hung by the head with rope along the bed frame. Maddy called out her name in disbelief and begged her to wake up but she didn't. His brother hated him for that, said he never desired to see him again and gave him an hour before he planned to get the police involved. Maddy was only 14 when he did this, just began high school and was already destined for failure with no support system and tears he couldn't manage to remove, not to mention no place to go.

He packed a bag of clothes and a few family photos he had as quick as possible, didn't even give his brother a proper goodbye, just went to the neighbour's house in a hurry who handed him many false documents he created for him as they brainstormed this plan for a while.

The neighbour was an elderly man who had connections and believed in being able to live a safe and happy life, what Maddy's dad prevented. He even dyed Maddy's naturally blonde hair to a dirty blonde with dark roots and provided him with different clothes to wear. His hair was never long but the elderly man provided him with extensions and he later began to grow it out on his own. This man had a nephew who lived in England and cleaned boats for a living. He got his nephew to agree to have Maddy help him with that job so he could support himself while still going to a new school nearby and having the luxury of living on whatever boat they were cleaning.

Maddy however was kicked off the boat the moment they began to clean the boats by the palace. Around this time, he saw a young girl who had a tendency to change near the window. She looked to be around his age and although he blocked himself off from emotion with girls after feeling as if his mom's death was his fault, that didn't take apart from the fact that he was a horny teenager. What he didn't know was that the boat cleaner had a daughter in the palace who was a servant and seamstress to princess Sophia. The girl whose curves, breasts, butt and everything in between Maddy practically drooled over was the boat cleaner's daughter.

The boat cleaner was a reasonable man who would've easily let this go but the fact that Maddy found a way to sneak into the palace to see her purely for the reason of her being the first girl he ever saw naked, pissed him off. Their secret stayed a secret for a while as she helped him push down any walls and barriers and helped him improve his grades in school and he added adventure to her simple life. Although, she began to change with her curtains in front of the window to avoid any conflict, her dad did go by the palace into her room the time her and Maddy were intimate for the first time ever.

Maddy tried explaining that there was so much more to their relationship than that but the boat cleaner was too close-minded that he fired Maddy who built his own boat and caught fish for a living while still seeing Gloria when he could until she wanted to settle down. He wasn't ready for that but his brother was who desired revenge on Maddy for destroying their family.

Since he parted ways from Gloria, no tears exited his cheeks. He wouldn't let them exit because from his experience, any time he cried, he had nobody to console him, so why bother?

Nolan's familiar eyes drew me to Maddy's experiences as if he was them because he was. It quickly made sense why I could see him and nobody else could. That was Harmony's miscarriage, the child he'll always be a father to emotionally and because of my close connection to Maddy, Nolan felt like my child too in a sense.

But with everything I saw that day, did Nolan vanish completely as if I already saw too much, as if Maddy would come back to me to tell me the rest.

Nolan hardly directly told me things about Maddy, was mainly there for me to have someone to talk so freely with. Yet I only saw the boy for a week before I saw part of Maddy's life through him. Morine wasn't truly there either. I like to believe she was an angel that guided the spirit of Nolan to me temporarily.

After he took off without so much as a goodbye, I went through the motions as I had been except with zero attitude. This was even the case towards Anderson who showed up to brag about his recent engagement and how that could've been me.

I wasn't planning to go backwards. I was promised on my 25th birthday that if I progressed well that I would be able to explore more than my room and the connected bathroom, but other residents who were in a similar mindset to me.

It was difficult to not think about Anderson since nobody had a way of boiling my blood as much as he had, but the idea of a cake and interacting with people that weren't nurses or in Heaven, made it easier to toss him aside.

However, it was as if God had other plans for me for my 25th birthday. The night prior, around ten when I was told to have my lights out, did the fire alarm go off. This wasn't the kind of place to do drills for obvious reasons and residents weren't allowed to handle anything fatal. Unless a resident pulled the alarm, it was a real fire and that was how they treated it.

An announcement circulated the building, telling the staff to unlock all the doors and remove handcuffs from anyone if applicable. I hadn't been in handcuffs in a long time, just needed my door unlocked which didn't take long as we were beyond overstaffed.

The cold, white, marble floor touched my bare feet as I threw my white bedspread off and instantly ran out of my dark room to the light in the hallway while staff guided us towards the nearest entrance and watched us closely.

A part of me desired to escape yet every time I was forced to leave, I left a little differently. I desired to catch glimpses of the girl I started as which that dull place allowed me to see when my true inner self was only displayed for me to see. Escaping would be changing and I felt like I wouldn't be able to look in the mirror with any more change.

A mirror was a weapon at this institution, so I hadn't looked at myself appearance wise in around seven years. My dark, wavy locks landed around my butt as someone who committed such a gruesome killing shouldn't be near any blade, that included scissors. As shaving went, I was only permitted to use wax strips, no blades. That was all I knew about my appearance but it didn't matter.

There isn't a mirror that exists that isn't already used. No image is original but the character behind the image is. I wasn't ready to look at the changed girl I still felt as if I hardly knew yet that perception changed fairly quickly.

My feet went from the cold, marble floor to the rocky cement ground, following the staff and the crowd. The blaring alarm took away from certain individuals screaming or attempting to disappear from the crowd as we waited for the fire department to arrive.

While staff fled to those individuals did I feel a blade graze my back. I didn't flinch or gaze behind me to see what was going on, just trusted that the end would feel peaceful light or dark and would make sense.

"Follow my lead and when I say run, run!" he whispered and my entire being fell to mush as the only life besides my own that mattered to me stripped me down when no eyes were on me. I let my white gown fall on the ground along with my undergarments to avoid taking any possible tracking devices with me while Maddy replaced them with his black boxers I rolled up the waistband of to fit better and his loose beige tank top. Just when I was clueless how new clothes would get me out of a mental institution, did Maddy yell out, "This was a trap, they planted a bomb!" to freak everyone out, especially considering the fact that he planted an empty briefcase with a timer. This managed to get everyone all jumpy and the delusional to make a scene, providing Maddy with the chance to hold my hand in his and whisper the three letter word I so desperately needed to hear despite knowing escaping wasn't in my best interest.

We ran as fast as we could until we reached the main dock where many massive boats were parked. We stopped to catch our breaths and look at each other for the first time in seven years, much differently than when we first met.

Maddy looked exactly as I remembered him with his bronze skin, eyes that put the sea to shame and his dirty blonde hair with walnut roots. The only difference was the fact that he had a beard and a scar above his lip.

His eyes sank far below the depths of my own. I couldn't help but faintly smile and his own subtle smile met my own before he pulled out a small, silver metal detector he grazed my body with before suggesting to head in the water fast in case anyone followed us.

He held his hand in my own, our fingers interlacing as we swam as one towards the bottom of the sea, my hair which was much longer than Maddy's for a change, clouded our vision which he gently pushed out of the way. He lifted up a metal lid and gestured for me to head inside the hole that revealed itself once its lid was pushed to the side.

My hands trembled as I faced the hole of the unknown but settled the moment I felt Maddy's hand on my back to indicate that I wasn't by myself in this new chapter. I closed my eyes to make it feel as if I awoke from a terrible slumber as I'd be seeing light whenever the dark tunnel ended. I told Maddy to warn me when it was over, when there was light at the end of the slumber. He told me I would just know, that the darkness I viewed with my eyes closed would have a glow to it that would tell me it was time to open them.

I didn't think that would be the case but trusted his judgement. I didn't see a glow in the darkness but felt what can be best compared to as a glow. For once, I didn't feel used, like the mirror I spent so much time in front of. I felt beautiful and recognized it officially because only he could make me feel that way. In his warmth, his arms, I finally understood it all.

That was the light, the glow. I found myself buried in his chest, skin to skin, no fabric minus the white comforter that reminded me of snow which we were snuggled close under. My lips still felt as if his were on them, that's how comforting his touch was and my entire body felt complete, being so close to him and it being obvious how intimate we got. He placed his hand on a faint bump on my stomach I was sensitive about as I pushed his hand away.

"I don't know how long we're safe for and I don't want this child to suffer because of our actions. What if we're found? They'd lose us. They'd have a bad start like we did and turn into us, maybe even kill…"

"That hole has no recognition of time once you're past your teen years. It was supposed to be a myth but I did my research and it's real, gives you the life you're entitled to even based on your worst mistakes, regrets and upbringing. This is where the universe wants us to be. We're in a secluded part of Florida and have beach days all year, that's the relaxation we deserve and although we were put here as if this was always our life, I want to have a family I choose. And I want that to be you and our baby that we'll make sure never is left behind and is always loved no matter what happens," he interrupted me to reassure me yet I was still slightly hesitant.

"We just got here. Even if this is where we're supposed to be and how right it feels, how do I know I won't be alone with our child?" I asked him in concern as I rubbed my hands in his mid-length hair that was longer than my freshly trimmed hair that landed past my ears like it had when it first fell out.

"You do remember I was next to you and Andy for the Law project?" Maddy asked me curiously as he brushed the side of my face with the palm of his hand, our eyes not leaving each other's along with the familiarity I always noticed with Maddy.

"That's kind of hard to forget," I sighed in frustration as to why he was bringing up yet another guy who shattered my heart like a mirror that could do severe damage. He continued to stroke my cheeks with his knuckles to tell me that he wasn't trying to upset me and even brushed his foot against my bare thigh to soothe me in an intimate way.

"Good because I was squished and never fell asleep since I needed to temporarily mark your legs. I know all he does about you except I actually listened and my heart tells me that the world can wait for its justice when I have you. That's what is right and you'll teach our kid right from wrong and that's better than any lawyer in my opinion," Maddy explained sweetly as he planted a gentle kiss on my head.

"Why kiss me three times, twice on the lips and once on the cheek, and not tell then?" I teased him, desiring to hear it although I already knew the answer.

"I had my theories about Harmony and that comfort, warmth and safety with you was all that felt real. I didn't care about Andy asshole or not, I knew what I felt and wanted to see if you felt it too. That's why I pushed you two together to see if I was imagining things between us and I kissed you to double check. It's stupid and I was selfish, and…"

"Kiss me a fourth time and I'll kiss you back. I'm sure we have before since we clearly made love but I want to remember it and not just feel it," I admitted to him, feeling giddy for the first time with him as it wasn't until we were apart that I knew he was much more than a friend.

"I love you, Viola. I love how I never have to explain myself with you. I love how you want to change this crappy world. I love how you've been cracked so many times but never broke, that's how strong you are," he whispered to me in a soft, angelic voice as he smothered his lips against my own, allowing my body to burn up as he slowly moved his lips further down shortly after I embraced the kiss.

"Nothing's ever felt more right than you, Maddy. I wish I realized it then and spent all the time I had with Anderson, with you. But things worked out as they were meant to and I love how protective you get around me, how you try to save someone who is no damsel, love how you created a life for yourself and are so brave and strong, and I love you," I managed to say three words that I never said to the right man until that day.

I remember him taking my hand in his and putting a thin gold ring on my pinky finger with half of a golden apple in the middle. He put a thicker ring on his pinky finger that looked much more masculine but still had half an apple in the middle.

"I want to be your husband before I really know what your body feels like in my own," he proposed in his own bad ass way that made my entire body go numb at the idea of choosing to spend the rest of my life with someone that gave it so much meaning. The idea of feeling warmth that exceeded his arms and lips alone was exciting yet terrifying as I'd feel all of him physically that I haven't discovered emotionally.

"I know I'm blushing but remove that smirk of yours because a wedding doesn't happen overnight," I teased him as I gently stroked my foot against his thigh.

"So, that's a yes then?" Maddy questioned me and I couldn't help but giggle.

"That was a question I didn't have to think about the answer twice to. But I didn't say that directly since you didn't ask traditionally and even put the ring on my pinky, not my ring finger," I admitted honestly.

"I thought that fit us since all the promises made to us from others were always broken, but not this, not us, ever, no matter what happens. And your birthmark you vaguely mentioned once didn't predict your future, you created it but our centres make us who we are and connect us, not the apple people first gaze at. And if you look at the bedside table, you know why we can never legally be married," he voiced to me in a thoughtful manner.

I glanced at fake IDs on the wooden bedside table which meant our marriage wouldn't be legal, so why have the ceremony at all?

"I had one illegal marriage and kissed him the same day, trying to push myself to feel this magical feeling that made poverty worth it for my lesbian aunts in an area where women needed to rely on men. I had one lustful moment with him, that was it. The palace life wasn't me and I wanted to leave. I didn't leave in the way I hoped but I was told I had a choice to leave at 18 if I didn't want to legalize the marriage. I'll never have the chance to be in a legal marriage but I want one to start off from love, like that one never did. So, we can do things backwards, make love and then dance, but I want the white dress that I get to pick, a bouquet I'll dry out to remember that day and you there with me in a suit, no pirate or casual clothes. We deserve a fairytale too and I want to start things off all fancied up because there is so much more to us than what people have read in the papers," I explained to him, his eyes not leaving my own for a second as his words said nothing but actions said everything as he whisked me away under the covers, making me feel as carefree as my childhood should've felt.

Maddy however didn't stop with the fast yet savoury motions that brought me to a place where only we existed and nothing or nobody else mattered. He left both me and himself breathless as I laid my head on his chest, listening to his heart thump as loudly as my heavy breaths.

"So, do you want to enjoy the aftermath a little longer or I can make you the wedding dress of your dreams? That's probably the only good thing that came out of my relationship with Gloria," he said sweetly and I faintly smiled at him which he returned.

"I just want to lie here all day with you but as soon as nightfall comes, we can start customizing the dress," I replied excitedly.

"That sounds nice," said Maddy in a soft tone his naturally deep voice had a habit in finding around me. "What do you think that star looks like?" he gestured towards the beige ceiling that quickly filled with twinkling lights best known as stars.

"That star to the left looks like an outcast, put to the side from the rest but that isn't a bad thing like it once thought, like she once thought," I exchanged a smile with him, teeth and all.

"Yeah, and the shooting star was so used to running with a big bang behind but this one will land on the surface of the earth and disintegrate as if it was never there, give it a bit of time. But it knows the outcast star knows it was there, saw it when everyone was staring at her and that's all that matters," he added some thoughtful words while he called me beautiful and said how if he knew life would be like this, his years leading up to this, his traumatic childhood would revolve around much less suffering.

That's always how it goes though. Is it not? We undergo scrapes, bruises, broken bones, some that leave marks that never vanish, some we can only see. We continue to rise above them because we don't know much better than that as we're constantly told that it will get better, will be worth it. Yet we never know for sure and that's why it can be so hard to follow through and not end life then and there or give up, sometimes temporarily but more often completely.

One can't erase black from what was once pure, darkness from what was once light. Even if erased, the residue will never vanish and will be there for eternity. That residue follows you and makes it more difficult to continue going but as you fall, you find pieces of yourself you never really took notice of before. You forget what your flesh truly looks like until all the splattered hearts of your life are removed when someone understands that hearts are meant to be whole, yours in particular.

Until then, you use your scattered pieces to help you grow. Success is best found in times of despair and sorrow. This is the same recipe for vengeance. It's easy to get tempted by revenge but then your darkness feels heavier than before since you haven't grown from your experiences, just felt them, haven't used them to live.

Things do change in time. We don't know if it's a good change but we can only hope. What was once innocent and good can become evil as one who understands my story knows. But darkness can also become bright, what most cease to see. My dark core doesn't make me who I am but the light that shines on it, the light I chose even if it's difficult to see, does.

Those used mirrors that never saw me, finally did by opening a door I thought I desired to close. Trust is fragile, like glass, like mirror shards. Once broken, it's beyond repair yet the stars, clouds, candy, real life sheep we could count and so much more in the ceiling told me otherwise.

We were safe and although what I first quickly glanced at thinking was our false identification was our real IDs we hid from everyone with our fresh starts yet told each other, I didn't believe my eyes. It wasn't until I noticed a young boy with amber orange hair and ocean blue eyes, who looked to be a toddler at most approach our home, banging the front and being pulled away from it by his mom.

"Teddy, let's not break the mirror, alright, honey. We can read more of *Shattered* tonight and you'll understand villains don't exist and mirrors shouldn't be played with," she told him in a sweet sing song tune, not being able to see in, only having us see out unless we desired to change that.

While looking out, I took notice of a novel that was in the palm of her hands that was completely dark but shined bright in the light as it read the title I called my journal to keep me sane in the institution. I don't know how it got out there, how we even got to a safe place that used to be anything but that looking in from the other side but didn't care.

My story was out in the world where it belongs. Even if only those two people read it, it's two more people who see past the labels in the world. This was when I knew what starts with broken trust, ends safe in warm arms with a child in my belly I knew would find a way to see that boy, glass in the way or not. I could happily say the fantasy land, land where one could wonder for ages how endless it is, how much there is to do without hiding and only being with those you care about most, wasn't being trapped.

Being trapped was being unhappy. If you're not happy, not satisfied, it isn't the end. You can be put in a bubble your entire life and carried in that bubble from place to place and still never be happy although all is figured out for you. The bubble isn't yet popped, what you need to do to feel free and then discover your own bubble that makes life worth living.

There is no such thing as villains and heroes both receiving what they deserve. If we continue to let labels define us, define what makes us unique and ourselves, we won't truly understand ourselves and all that life is meant to be. We'll only ever survive and not live every moment, every minute, every second, feeling all there is to feel, taking in every ounce and crying real tears of happiness, no more blood, no more pain, for now. We wouldn't be put in a world with so many people to change our lives if we were only meant to get by it day by day and take nothing out of it.

Instead of thinking of yourself as good or bad, think of qualities that you like in yourself and some you're not as fond of. Use those good ones as reasons why you belong in this world and those not so great ones as reasons to keep moving, to get better.

Not all endings to one chapter that begin another are perfect but they fit the story you create for yourself, no one else. As one mirror shatters, as blood sheds, tears escape, your heart pounds, you find yourself trapped again and again, keep moving forward. You, yourself, don't always have the answer and sometimes feeling, observing, waiting and most importantly, hoping, result in a path you never predicted or expected to curve your direction which is within reach for a change.

About the Author

Julia Vellucci

Julia Vellucci is a 19-year-old girl, born and raised in Mississauga, Ontario, with eight romance books, a fantasy novella as well as an anthology published, and a passion for the written craft. She is Italian by origin. She has never been good at visual art but her mom and younger sister both of whom she admires are definitely her creative endeavours as she was inspired by them to find a way to express her creative side, through writing. She discovered her love for creative writing about three years ago when she first began to bring fictional characters to life through the written craft thanks to a school book club she was part of and couldn't help but wanted to discover what made her characters unique and carry out their story until the very end. Julia's dream is to be able to inspire readers through her words as she believes words can project more than actions ever could.

Readers can visit her website at *juliavellucci.weebly.com* and find her on Instagram under the username *juliavelluciauthor*.

www.ingramcontent.com/pod-product-compliance
Lightning Source LLC
LaVergne TN
LVHW041929070526
838199LV00051BA/2754